Enjoy all of these American Girl Mysteries®:

THE SILENT STRANGER   A *Kaya* Mystery

LADY MARGARET'S GHOST   A *Felicity* Mystery

SECRETS IN THE HILLS   A *Josefina* Mystery

THE HIDDEN GOLD   A *Marie-Grace* Mystery

THE RUNAWAY FRIEND   A *Kirsten* Mystery

SHADOWS ON SOCIETY HILL   An *Addy* Mystery

CLUES IN THE CASTLE TOWER   A *Samantha* Mystery

THE CRYSTAL BALL   A *Rebecca* Mystery

MISSING GRACE   A *Kit* Mystery

CLUES IN THE SHADOWS   A *Molly* Mystery

THE SILVER GUITAR   A *Julie* Mystery

*and many more!*

— A *Cécile* MYSTERY —

# THE CAMEO
# NECKLACE

by Evelyn Coleman

★ American Girl®

PICTURE CREDITS
The following individuals and organizations have generously
given permission to reprint illustrations contained in "Looking Back":
pp. 156–157—swamp scene, Thomas Moran, *Slave Hunt, Dismal Swamp, Virginia,*
1862. Gift of Laura A. Clubb, 1947.8.44. © 2011 Philbrook Museum of Art, Inc.,
Tulsa, Oklahoma (detail); portrait, Photographs and Prints Division, Schomburg
Center for Research in Black Culture, The New York Public Library, Astor, Lenox
and Tilden Foundations (detail); pp. 158–159—cypress swamp, Morris Museum
of Art, Augusta, Georgia (detail); chains, courtesy of the Drain Collection;
swamp hideout, Photographs and Prints Division, Schomburg Center for
Research in Black Culture, The New York Public Library, Astor, Lenox and Tilden
Foundations; cypress basket, photo, Thomas Wintz, courtesy Louisiana Folklife
Program; pp. 160–161—French Market, North Wind Picture Archives; run-
away, North Wind Picture Archives; Black Seminoles, courtesy of Bonnie Peters
Gearhart, Groveland, Florida; pp. 162–163—Jamaican bill, © Bank of Jamaica;
courtyard, courtesy of Teri Robida; portrait, Photographs and Prints Division,
Schomburg Center for Research in Black Culture, The New York Public Library,
Astor, Lenox and Tilden Foundations (detail); paper, The Historic New Orleans
Collection; Floating Palace circus, Collection of The New-York Historical Society,
ID 36805.

Author photo by Sue Ann Kuhn-Smith/Newton Citizen

Illustrations by Sergio Giovine

Cataloging-in-Publication Data
available from the Library of Congress

*To my youngest daughter, my talented reader,
Latrayan (Sankofa) Mueed, who helps me become a better
writer with each book. And to the man who endures
months of being ignored for the sake of my writing,
my "rock," my wonderful husband, Talib Din.*

*I also want to dedicate this book to the ancestors and to
all the descendants of the maroons, the escaped enslaved,
and those who were not able to escape . . . and to the
men, women, and children massacred at Fort Negro.
Always remember our fight for freedom!*

# TABLE OF CONTENTS

1 A NIGHT AT THE CIRCUS . . . . . . . . . . . . 1

2 CONFUSION ON THE WHARF . . . . . . . 12

3 UNCLE HENRY'S LAST GIFT . . . . . . . . 22

4 BACK TO THE FLOATING PALACE . . . . . 31

5 CLOSE CALL . . . . . . . . . . . . . . . . . . . 46

6 AN UNEXPECTED INVITATION . . . . . . . 53

7 THE FRENCH MARKET . . . . . . . . . . . . 62

8 TROUBLING QUESTIONS . . . . . . . . . . . 73

9 HUNTERS AND LIONS . . . . . . . . . . . . . 82

10 MISS MILLIE . . . . . . . . . . . . . . . . . . . 90

11 AGNÈS'S SURPRISE . . . . . . . . . . . . . . . 98

12 MESSAGE IN CONGO SQUARE . . . . . . 112

13 CHASE . . . . . . . . . . . . . . . . . . . . . . . 120

14 HANNAH'S SECRET . . . . . . . . . . . . . . 130

15 SHADOWS IN THE NIGHT . . . . . . . . . 143

   LOOKING BACK . . . . . . . . . . . . . . . . 156

   GLOSSARY OF FRENCH WORDS . . . . . 164

# 1

# A NIGHT AT THE CIRCUS

**November 1854**

Cécile Rey's heart pounded in her chest, louder than a blacksmith's hammer. She held her breath. She could feel perspiration slipping down her face, even though the gas lamps on the ornate walls of the *Floating Palace* showboat gave out little warmth to dispel the night's chill. Cécile was squeezing her fists so tight, her nails created indentations in her palms. The man teetering on the tightrope swayed too far to the right. *"Mon Dieu!"* she breathed. "Good heavens."

Cécile had never seen anything so thrilling in her eleven-year-old life. She glanced quickly at her friend, Monette Bruiller, and wondered if Monette was experiencing the same strange mix of feelings she was—scared to look, but wanting to see it all. Cécile turned back, pinning her eyes to the man dancing on the wire, as if by force of will she could catch him if he fell.

The circus acts were so exhilarating! The acrobats flipped and tumbled. The jugglers threw rings and clubs high in the air and to each other without ever dropping anything. The animals stood on their hind legs, jumped through hoops, and danced, and even the most ferocious appeared tame. Clowns mimed, pranced, and had the audience laughing. A real band, dressed in bright red uniforms with gold braid and shiny buttons, played lively songs to accompany every act. And then there was the finale.

Cécile watched a white horse thunder around the huge ring. A man sat atop the bareback horse. Suddenly he vaulted upward and planted his feet on the horse's back. He balanced there on the galloping horse, his knees bent. Then, without warning, he was sailing through the air.

Cécile grabbed her throat. She felt alone,

as if the crowd had disappeared and there was no one but her watching the scene unfolding on the stage far below. The sounds of shuffling bodies and whispered chatter fell away. As the man flipped upward, the only noise was the faint sound of the horse's pounding hooves. Then, to Cécile's astonishment, the man turned a somersault in the air and landed smoothly on the back of the horse!

Seconds ticked by before the spectators found their voices and the room filled with boisterous cheers. Cécile rose from her seat, still dazed. She looked around. All the other free people of color were on their feet, too. Like the rest of the crowd, Cécile broke into frenzied clapping.

The circus performers were gathered in the ring now, bowing to the crowd. Cécile sat down again and leaned over the edge of the balcony as far as she could to get a better look. The scene below was breathtaking—the silk and velvet curtains flowing, all the performers in plumes of feathers, sparkling costumes, elaborate head-dresses. It was like a fairy tale.

Cécile turned her attention briefly to the audience down below, closer to the ring, where the white people sat. She wondered if they could see the faces of the performers better, or hear them speaking to one another in their different languages. Cécile knew that many who worked for the circus came from distant parts of the world, places that Grand-père, her grandfather, had visited as a sailor. It was at moments like this that Cécile wished the free people of color could sit in any seat they could afford.

Someone tugged Cécile's sleeve. It was Agnès Metoyer. She was poised on Cécile's right side, holding dainty binoculars up to her eyes.

"If you'd brought opera glasses, you would have had more fun," Agnès said.

"You can look through mine," Fanny Metoyer offered, reaching around Agnès and holding her glasses out to Cécile.

"We're not supposed to let anyone borrow them," Agnès said, pulling her sister's arm back. "Remember?"

Fanny shrugged to Cécile. "Sorry."

Monette, standing on Cécile's left, leaned toward the Metoyer sisters. "She wouldn't be borrowing them—you'd just let her use them for a minute, that's all."

"That's borrowing," Agnès replied.

"It doesn't matter," Cécile said. "I can see very well, thank you." She didn't want to borrow anything from Agnès Metoyer. Agnès never treated her very nicely.

"What an exquisite necklace you're wearing, Cécile," Monette said, leaning closer for a better look.

Cécile reached up to feel the necklace, an ivory cameo—a side view of a woman's face—with a rose diamond placed where an earring would be. The cameo was set on a circular ruffle of black lace, attached to a black ribbon. The necklace looked very grown-up. It belonged to Cécile's Aunt Octavia, whom she called Tante Tay.

"Let me see it," Agnès said. She lifted the cameo, examining it carefully. "It is beautiful," she said after a moment. "Is that a real diamond?"

"Yes," Cécile replied proudly.

"I like it," said Fanny.

"It would look lovely on me," Agnès said, reaching her hand out again. "Let me try it on."

Monette chimed in. "Cécile's not supposed to let anyone borrow it," she said. With a broad grin, she added, "Right, Cécile?"

Agnès said, "I wasn't going to . . ." Then her voice trailed off. Cécile and Monette exchanged amused glances. Evidently Agnès realized that she'd been caught, because she said quietly, "Never mind."

A moment later, Cécile's tutor, Monsieur Lejeune, joined the girls. He and his sister, Mademoiselle Lejeune, had taken Cécile and Monette to the circus as a reward for doing well in their studies. The Lejeunes had picked up both girls in a hired carriage, but they had sat a few rows behind them at the performance so that Cécile and Monette could sit with the Metoyer sisters.

At first Cécile had wanted to explain that she and Monette weren't really friends with the sisters. But then Cécile was glad she hadn't said

6

anything, because sitting without chaperones had felt more grown-up.

"Ladies, ladies, did you enjoy the show?" Monsieur Lejeune asked as he put on his gloves.

"*Oui*, Monsieur Lejeune. Oh, yes!" Cécile and Monette said, beginning to describe their favorite parts.

"*Très bien*, very good. You'll have to tell me all about it later. Right now, we need to catch a carriage before they're all taken. Follow me."

Cécile and Monette filed out behind the Lejeunes, joining the river of people trying to make their way off the showboat onto the wharf. The Lejeunes were in front, pushing the way forward. The crush of people moved like a school of fish, no space between them, all headed in the same direction—through the doors of the showboat, down the plank, and onto the wharf. Once on the ground, the river of people flowed into an ocean of circus-goers, sailors, and people out on the town on Saturday night.

Shoved this way and that by the crowd,

Cécile realized that every few steps, she seemed to fall farther behind Monette and the Lejeunes. She wished she'd grabbed Monette's hand, even if it would have made her feel like a little girl.

Now Cécile could barely see the back of Monette's head as she moved in the crush of the crowd on the wharf. The smells and calls from the *marchands* selling treats caught Cécile's attention as she found herself pushed toward the edge of the crowd. On one side of her, a tall, aproned man with a reddish beard was holding a tray aloft and calling out, "Hot orange buns! Hot, sweet orange buns!" On Cécile's other side, two children about her age with flowing black hair and light brown skin held up woven baskets and yelled, "Get the last cypress baskets. Last ones. Hurry, last chance." The baskets were beautiful. Cécile had never seen baskets with indigo-blue stripes.

A very short woman with tiny blond ringlets pressed close to the marchands. Cécile's eyes widened as she noticed that the woman was wearing a purple and gold circus costume; a band around her head held a matching plume of purple and gold feathers. Cécile's heart sped up. Maybe she could meet a real circus performer! Before she could speak to the woman, Cécile felt a tap on her shoulder. She turned and found herself looking at Agnès and Fanny Metoyer and one of their servant boys.

"Hello again," Agnès said. She reached out and touched Cécile's necklace. "I do so love this necklace."

"*Merci.* Thank you," Cécile said. She turned to face forward again, trying to see Monette and the Lejeunes. At that moment, she noticed a shabby old woman coming toward her, making her way against the crowd. The colorful *tignon* knotted around the woman's head bobbed up and down as she moved through the throng.

The tall marchand reached out over the crowd to the old woman as he called, "Get your orange buns. Hot orange buns!"

Suddenly he lost his balance. He crashed into Cécile, who lost her footing and fell, knocking the old woman down.

"Oh, *madame*, I am so sorry!" cried Cécile, now sprawled on the wharf beside the old woman. The stacks of orange buns rained down around them, followed closely by the crashing tray. The two children selling baskets scrambled to pick up the buns, even grabbing a few that had landed in Cécile's lap. The Metoyer sisters looked on as their servant picked up buns next to Cécile. The tall man reached over Cécile's head and snatched up his tray.

Cécile looked at the old woman with concern. "Are you all right?" she asked.

Despite the chaos, the old woman reached out, her bangles and bracelets shifting as she grasped Cécile's wrist. She pulled Cécile closer, as if she were going to say something.

The blonde circus performer leaned over them, her drawstring purse dangling in Cécile's face, and asked, "Is either of you hurt?"

Suddenly, only a few feet from the spilled group, a passerby hugging a bottle slurred loudly, "Somebody picked my pocket!" The crowd around him began jostling as men checked their pockets and women secured or felt for their jewelry.

Cécile started to feel for her necklace but found herself being yanked up by the old woman, whose grip was surprisingly strong.

"Merci. I am so sorry for knocking you down," Cécile said, hastily straightening her dress and cloak. She was about to make sure the old woman was all right but realized that she was no longer beside her.

As quickly as the old woman had disappeared, Cécile found herself being moved along by a new crush of people emerging from the showboat. Anxiously Cécile rose on tiptoe, attempting to catch a glimpse of Monette or the Lejeunes.

At the same time, Cécile reached up to feel for her necklace. Her fingers grasped air.

Panic exploded in her chest. The necklace she had borrowed from her aunt was gone.

# 2

## CONFUSION ON THE WHARF

Cécile's heart raced; she could hear it pounding. She had to find that necklace.

She turned and tried to retrace her steps to the spot where she had fallen. She put both arms out, attempting to part the sea of people still streaming down the wharf. They were so close, Cécile could smell on their breath the foods they'd eaten. She could hear bits of conversations, laughter, an argument or two. Looking down, she frantically checked the ground as she moved against the flow of the crowd, but she saw nothing. "Excuse me," she shouted. "Did anyone see my necklace?" People ignored her or shook their heads no.

When had she lost it? She'd had it on only moments before, when Agnès had greeted her and touched the necklace. Then she'd fallen.

For a second, Cécile thought she heard her name being called, but she ignored it. Only one thing mattered now—she had to get back to the spot where she had fallen to see if she could find Tante Tay's necklace.

"*Pardon*. Excuse me," Cécile said, alternating between French and English. She shoved against the crowd, but its movement was strong and she was still being pushed forward, away from the spot where she'd fallen.

A surge of fear shot through her: What if the pickpocket that the passerby was yelling about had taken it? No—Cécile would not allow herself to think that. The necklace *had* to be there, right where she'd fallen.

In desperation, Cécile dropped onto her hands and knees and began crawling through the crowd. "Ouch!" she cried as someone stepped on her fingers. She felt the squish of something nasty, a wad of tobacco that someone had spit out, and realized she'd forgotten her gloves again. She wiped her palm, now caked with dirt, on her cloak.

Cécile kept moving through the crowd, still saying, "Excuse me." When she saw a few trampled buns, she knew she was in the right place. She swept her hands back and forth across the dirt but found nothing.

Cécile hopped up, calling out over and over, "Has anyone seen my necklace?"

Finally she stopped. She looked out over the crowd surging by and realized that not only had she lost the necklace, she had lost the Lejeunes and Monette too. They were nowhere in sight. The crowd was thick, festive, and constantly shifting. Cécile was alone.

She had to think clearly. What should she do?

She decided she must keep looking for Tante Tay's necklace. It must have come off when she fell. If she didn't find it now, she might never get it back. Had someone picked it up after it slipped from her neck? Cécile studied the faces of the people nearby.

The tall marchand who had dropped the tray of buns was standing over to her right. Now he held the empty tray at his side. He was looking downward, concentrating on his right hand. Had he picked up the necklace?

Just as Cécile started to push her way toward him, she caught sight of a plume of purple and gold feathers. It belonged to the blonde woman in the circus costume—and she was even closer. Cécile shifted direction. "Excuse me. Pardon," she murmured, keeping her eye on the performer, who was now busy tucking something into her jeweled drawstring purse, the same one that had dangled near Cécile's face.

But the crowd's momentum propelled her slightly to the left, and instead Cécile found herself right in front of the old woman she'd accidentally knocked down.

The old woman was leaning against the wall of a warehouse, staring at Cécile. She clenched a strange, elaborately carved wooden pipe in her mouth. Her brown face was angular and weathered, and long tufts of gray hair fell loose from her tignon. Abruptly she stopped looking at Cécile and stared off into the crowd, nodding.

Cécile turned, following the old woman's gaze, and spotted the two young basket sellers, their hair loosely flowing around their shoulders. One of them held a cluster of cypress baskets, each one striped with indigo. For a brief moment, they looked in Cécile's direction, their large, slanting eyes dark and piercing in their long thin faces. The two looked so much alike, Cécile wondered whether they were boys or girls. They began moving toward her swiftly, bobbing and weaving through the crowd as smoothly as water snakes in a river.

Cécile held her breath. The children were heading right for her. Did they have her necklace?

She jumped as a hand grasped her shoulder. "Here you are," Monsieur Lejeune exclaimed, gently turning her toward him. "Thank heavens! I thought we'd lost you. Come with me. Mademoiselle Lejeune and Monette are waiting for us near the carriages."

"I'm so sorry, monsieur. Please, wait just a moment—" Cécile began. But her words were swallowed up by the boom of a cannon. Cécile knew this was the signal to warn that it was nine o'clock and all the slaves needed to be off the streets. She glanced back over her shoulder, but the two children were gone.

Before Cécile could say more, Monsieur Lejeune took her hand, pulling her urgently through the crowd. Cécile pressed her lips together, trying not to cry. She had lost her chance to find out if the children had her necklace, or to question the other people who had been near her when she fell.

As she and Monsieur Lejeune inched forward in the crowd, Cécile caught sight of the old woman standing a few feet ahead. How had she gotten there so fast?

"Monsieur Lejeune, may I stop for a moment to speak to that lady ahead?" Cécile asked. "I knocked her down earlier by accident, and I didn't apologize properly."

"All right, but hurry, please. I'll wait right over there, where I can see Monette and my sister waiting for the carriage. Please don't tarry."

Cécile rushed over to the old woman,

surprised at how easily she reached her. She could see now that the old woman was barefoot, even though it was cold outside. Had she lost her shoes when she fell?

The old woman's eyes met Cécile's, almost as if she'd been expecting her return. The woman took the pipe from her mouth. "You are searching for something very valuable," she said, reaching out to touch Cécile's face. Her fingers felt cold and ironlike as they stroked Cécile's cheek.

Cécile's thoughts raced. The woman *must* have the necklace—how else would she know that something of value was missing? Excitedly, Cécile asked, "You found my necklace?"

The old woman gave Cécile a long look. "No," she said gently. "It is your heart that you must find."

Cécile flushed as if she were standing too near a hot cookstove. She didn't understand what the old woman was talking about.

"As for your necklace," the old woman went on, "those we cannot know have it." Without warning, she grasped Cécile's hands. Cécile tried to pull away, but the old woman's grip was strong. Cécile looked around, frantic. She caught sight of Monsieur Lejeune, but he was staring out over the crowd toward the carriage stop. The old woman drew Cécile's hands toward her, palms up. Staring at Cécile's palms, she said almost in a whisper, "Remember, hunters always want to kill lions . . . Lions only want to eat."

Cécile felt tears pushing out of the corners of her eyes. She was frightened, and she wasn't sure why. The old woman let go of her hands and pointed up to the sky. Cécile's eyes followed the motion, noticing the woman's wrinkled hand, the many jangling bracelets on her wrist, and all the rings on her fingers.

The old woman's hand moved in front of Cécile's face in a circular motion, as if to include the crowd, the warehouses, and the ships that lined the wharves. "Open your eyes, girl," she said. "Open your eyes so you can see."

"I *can* see," Cécile whispered, feeling a tightening in her stomach.

"Not yet," the old woman said, moving her hand so close to Cécile's forehead that she could feel the air stirring. "Not yet."

Cécile felt as if she were falling again. Her body tensed and she closed her eyes, whispering, "But I can see."

When she opened her eyes, only Monsieur Lejeune was standing beside her. "Are you all right?" he asked. "Who are you talking to?"

Just then a woman screamed, "Thieves! Thieves!"

Cécile and everyone else looked in the direction of the screams. They seemed to have come from a *marchande* selling popcorn balls and macaroons in front of one of the warehouses.

Cécile spotted two children racing toward the edge of the crowd. She recognized them as the children with the cypress baskets. Some of the men in the crowd tried to grab their threadbare cloaks, but no one caught them before they disappeared into the darkness.

When the commotion had settled, Monsieur Lejeune and Cécile made their way to the carriage. The word *thieves* rang in Cécile's ears as Monsieur Lejeune ushered Mademoiselle, Monette, and Cécile into a carriage. As she stepped inside, Cécile wondered if those two children had the cameo necklace, and if they were the pickpockets and thieves making off with their prize.

And the old woman—whatever had she meant? *Those we cannot know have it ... Open your eyes so you can see ...* Cécile trembled with confusion and fear just thinking about the old woman and her words.

As the carriage jounced home, Cécile forced herself to join in the conversation around her, as Maman would expect her to. But her mind tumbled with the events of the evening—the marvels of the circus, the strange talk of the old woman, and, most of all, the awful misery of losing Tante Tay's necklace.

# 3
## UNCLE HENRY'S LAST GIFT

When Cécile arrived at her home on
Dumaine Street, she found her mother waiting
up for her. Promising to tell Maman all about
the circus in the morning, Cécile said good
night, rushed upstairs to her bedroom, and
closed the door.

Inside her room, alone at last, Cécile stared
at herself in the mirror, touching her neck where
the necklace had been only an hour before.
As she watched the tears slip down her face,
the true horror of losing the necklace stabbed
her heart.

Tante Tay had shown Cécile the beautiful
necklace a month ago, as Cécile helped her pack
for her first journey back to Philadelphia to visit
her in-laws since her husband, Uncle Henry, had

died. In the two years since Tante Tay had been widowed, she and her little son, René, had lived with Cécile's family, and Cécile had grown very close to her gentle young aunt.

Fingering the beautiful cameo, Cécile had nearly swooned. "Oh, Tante Tay, if you go someplace fancy on your trip, you will look so lovely in your necklace."

"Merci, Cécile," Tante Tay had said. "I do love wearing this necklace. One day I will let you wear it for a special occasion. Would you like that?"

"Oh, yes," Cécile had breathed. "That would be wonderful."

But instead of packing the necklace, Tante Tay had put it back in its velvet box and placed it in her drawer. She had explained that the necklace was the last gift Uncle Henry had given her. She would not chance taking it on the train with her for fear of losing it or having it stolen.

*I should have listened to what Tante Tay said,* Cécile thought now, crying harder. Instead, she had borrowed her aunt's necklace to wear just this one time to the fancy circus on the show-boat. She had not asked anyone's permission, reasoning that if Tante Tay had been home, she would have counted the circus as a special occasion and allowed her to wear the necklace.

Finally, Cécile got into bed, but she couldn't sleep. Tante Tay would be back from Philadelphia in just six days. She had to find the necklace before then—but how?

Unable to sleep, Cécile got up, threw on a shawl, and tiptoed out to the balcony. The moon was shining brightly, a few clouds speeding out of sight. The stars twinkled overhead. Cécile searched the sky for the Big Dipper. Somehow knowing it was in the sky always made her feel better. She did not hear a sound except a hooting owl in the distance.

Cécile tried to recall every detail about those few moments between the time she had last felt the necklace on her neck and the instant when she had discovered it was gone. As she did so, Cécile realized it was possible that no one had taken the necklace. Perhaps someone in the crowd had unknowingly stepped on it and crushed it into the dirt, and that's why Cécile hadn't seen it. Maybe it was still there on the wharf. Or maybe some honest person had picked it up and turned it in to the circus's Lost and Found. That was possible, too.

*Tomorrow,* she decided, *I must find a way to go back to the wharf and check.*

On the other hand, maybe someone *had* taken it. Cécile remembered each person who had been standing closest to her. She recalled them clearly: the man selling orange buns, the strange old woman, the Metoyer sisters and their servant, the blonde woman in the circus costume, the two children with the cypress baskets. Perhaps one of those people had picked up the necklace. Only the Metoyer sisters would have known it belonged to her.

Cécile squared her shoulders, shivering against the chilly night air. If she couldn't find it at the wharf, or in the circus's Lost and Found, she would track down every one of those people again, even the two children who might be thieves, to ask them about the necklace.

She had no choice if she was to find it before Tante Tay returned.

Cécile woke up early on Sunday morning. While she dressed, she thought about how she could get back to the wharf. It wouldn't be easy. Like any young lady, Cécile was not allowed to go out alone. What excuse could she give for asking someone to go back with her? She couldn't bear to tell Maman or Papa what had really happened. They would be so disappointed in her for wearing the necklace without her aunt's permission. She didn't even want to tell Grand-père or her brother, Armand.

Cécile wished that her dear friend Marie-Grace Gardner were in New Orleans. She and Marie-Grace had solved a lot of difficult problems together. But Marie-Grace was away, visiting relatives. Cécile was on her own. She took a deep breath and started downstairs.

The house was quiet except for the occasional clanging of pots as the cook, Mathilde, prepared breakfast in the kitchen building at the back of the courtyard. Cécile went into the parlor and lifted the cover from her parrot's cage. *"Bonjour,* Cochon," she said. "Wake up, sleepyhead."

Cochon ruffled his feathers and squawked, "Wake up! Wake up!"

"Cécile, what are you doing up so early?" Maman said, peering into the parlor. "Come, tell me about the circus while I water the flowers."

Out in the courtyard, walking alongside Maman, Cécile described the evening at the circus, leaving out what had happened with the necklace. She had just thought of an excuse she might give Maman for going back today when Hannah, the new housemaid, stepped into the garden.

"Good morning, madame. May I cut some

flowers for the breakfast table?" she asked.

"Yes, of course," Maman said.

As Hannah snipped roses behind them, Cécile continued talking. "Maman, you know my knitted blue gloves? I think I dropped them last night on the wharf. Is it all right if Armand walks me back there after church today?"

"Do you mean the gloves Grand-père bought you for Christmas?"

"Yes, those." Cécile bit her lip.

"Excuse me, madame," Hannah said.

*Oh no!* Cécile suddenly remembered that Hannah had helped her dress last night. Did she know that Cécile hadn't worn her gloves? Was she going to tell Maman?

But Hannah only said, "Madame, would you like more water in your pitcher?"

Relieved, Cécile watched Hannah carry Maman's pitcher to the cistern. Hannah, she reflected, was so different from their previous maid, Ellen, who had died in the terrible yellow fever epidemic last year. Ellen had been lively and funny, and she had liked to tell Cécile stories about her big Irish family. Hannah was quiet, and even though she was a free person of color like the Reys, she said little about herself. Yet just like Ellen, she seemed to know, without being told, exactly when something needed to be done. Hannah had been with them for several months, and Maman seemed pleased with her.

Cécile turned back to Maman. "May I go look for my gloves?"

"I think you should," Maman said. "They were so pretty. I hope no one has picked them up. Now you must have breakfast and get ready for church." Then Maman said to Hannah, "You should get ready, too. Your chores can wait. You said you would come this Sunday."

"I'm sorry, madame," Hannah replied, barely above a whisper. "I'm not feeling so well today. Maybe next Sunday."

At breakfast, Cécile listened to her mother tell Grand-père, Papa, and Armand that Cécile had lost her gloves.

Cécile felt terrible not telling the truth to her mother. She wished the story were true, that the gloves were all she'd lost last night! Cécile swallowed a lump in her throat. Losing her gloves wouldn't be at all like losing the last gift from someone's husband. Unlike the gloves, the necklace was irreplaceable.

As Cécile sat with her family in Saint Louis Cathedral later that morning, she prayed that when she went back to the *Floating Palace*, her necklace would be waiting safely in the Lost and Found, or even lying in the dirt. *Please just let me find it,* she prayed. For the rest of Mass, Cécile counted the minutes until she was free to go and search.

# 4
## BACK TO THE FLOATING PALACE

When Mass ended, Cécile burst through the heavy cathedral doors, anxious to get back to the wharf. Armand was right beside her. "You seem awfully worried about your gloves," he said. "Let's go and find them."

Cécile and her brother set off for the wharf almost in silence. Usually they would have talked the whole way, but today he seemed preoccupied, and Cécile was lost in thought, too. The overcast sky seemed to reflect their mood.

They had almost passed Jackson Square when Armand stopped to read a handbill nailed to a tree. Cécile waited, so deep in thought about the necklace that she barely noticed the people strolling on the square. But then she spotted Monsieur Lejeune on a side street, his head bent down as he talked with a woman under a tree.

Cécile was about to go greet her tutor when he hurried off. The woman he'd been talking to turned and walked toward the cathedral. Cécile squinted. Why, it was Hannah. Cécile was glad to think she must be feeling better. Cécile knew that her tutor and Hannah were acquainted. Maman had said that Monsieur Lejeune was the one who had told Hannah the Reys needed a housemaid and suggested she apply.

"Come on, Cécé. I just saw something that will make you happy," Armand said, grabbing her hand. "We have to hurry."

Cécile doubted that anything could make her happy until she found Tante Tay's necklace, but she allowed her big brother to pull her along. Now he seemed just as anxious to get to the circus as she did.

They hurried down to the levee. A few people were strolling or riding in carriages, but the crowds and marchands were gone. They easily found the *Floating Palace* among the dozens of steamboats lined up along the wharves, their smokestacks releasing dark plumes into the air.

Armand pointed to a small wooden booth near the showboat. "That's where they sell tickets to the circus," he said. "The Lost and Found is probably there, too. Go see, and when you're done, come over here." Armand gestured to one of the nearby warehouses. "I have a surprise for you."

Cécile hurried to the ticket booth. A sign said the circus was closed on Sundays, and she didn't see anyone at the window. She stood on tiptoe and leaned over the ticket counter. Maybe she could at least see if there was a Lost and Found box inside.

"May I help you?" a voice roared.

Cécile was so startled, she almost fell backward. Behind the counter was the shortest man she'd ever seen. He reminded her of stories in *Harper's Monthly* magazine about a tiny circus man named General Tom Thumb.

"I said, may I help you?" he boomed again. Cécile wondered how on earth such a big voice

33

could be inside this little man. He held up his short-fingered hand. "Howdy. What can I do for you?"

Cécile reached across the counter and shook his hand. "Bonjour, *monsieur*. I lost a necklace. I thought maybe someone had turned it in. It was—"

"Stop," the man said, holding his hand up to his forehead. "Let me guess. Was it a beautiful pearl necklace?"

Cécile shook her head. "No, it was a cameo necklace on black lace."

The little man shrugged. "I'm better at guessing weights." He tilted his head. "Hmm, seventy-two pounds?"

Cécile had no idea how much she weighed, but she was beginning to feel that this conversation wasn't very helpful. Ignoring his guess, she asked, "Does the circus have a Lost and Found?"

The little man cackled. "Sure we do. You lose it, we find it—and then we keep it."

Cécile decided she was wasting time talking to him. "Thank you," she said, walking away.

"Sorry," he called after her. "Only joking with you. We have a Lost and Found, but no one turned in your necklace. Hope you find it."

Cécile thanked him again and scanned the wharf, looking for the spot where she had fallen. Yes, there it was—not far from the showboat's gangplank, off to the right where the marchands had stood. Cécile walked toward the spot, slowing her pace as she neared it. She surveyed the wharf with each step, but she didn't see the necklace. She didn't even see crumbs from the fallen orange buns. Birds or rats had probably cleaned them up.

Thunder rumbled in the distance. Cécile heard Armand calling her. She looked up to see an astonishing sight. Across the wharf, a young man was leading an elephant out of a warehouse—and Armand was walking beside them!

"Come here, Cécile," he shouted. "I have a surprise for you."

Cécile hurried to her brother, staring in amazement at the elephant.

Armand's face was lit up with satisfaction.

35

"Pierre here is going to let you ride the elephant!"

The huge animal stopped walking. Cécile was almost close enough to touch its side. The elephant was so much bigger than she had ever imagined. She felt like a small insect standing beside it.

"Ride the elephant?" Cécile's stomach lurched. She didn't want to ride an elephant. She only wanted to find her necklace!

"I saw a handbill advertising elephant rides," Armand explained. "Pierre says they don't give rides on Sundays—but for a generous tip, he'll make an exception for you." Armand winked.

Pierre said, "You can touch her if you want."

Cécile didn't want to touch her. The elephant wouldn't bring her aunt's necklace back.

"Her name is Bella," Pierre said. "She's very gentle. Go ahead."

Cécile remembered Grand-père telling her once that circus people considered it good luck to rub the neck of a giraffe. An elephant was even bigger. Maybe it would bring her luck, and she'd find the necklace.

Cécile reached out and touched the elephant's rough skin. "She has hair," Cécile said, surprised. She let her fingers glide along the ruffled, tough skin. Bella had folds near her knees, as if her skin were a bolt of cloth. The elephant moved her trunk slowly from side to side. Her tail swatted the air occasionally.

"Ready to ride?" Pierre asked, holding up a rope attached to Bella's harness.

Cécile shook her head. She needed to find the necklace.

"Come on, Cécé," Armand said. "This is the chance of a lifetime."

Cécile could see that her brother was proud to have gotten her this opportunity. She backed up a few steps. Did she dare ride an elephant? Maman would be horrified, but maybe Papa and Grand-père would think Cécile brave. Armand always said that he thought she was very brave.

Her heart pounded. She had to admit, this would be quite a story to tell Monette and Marie-Grace. She'd bet even the Metoyer sisters had never ridden an elephant.

Cécile said, "Oui, I will get on, but only for a moment." Then, she promised herself, she would get back to searching for the necklace as soon as she got off.

Pierre picked up a bale of hay and set it next to Bella. The elephant got down on her knees. Armand held Cécile's hand as she put one foot on the bale. Her stomach did a somersault. Could she actually do this?

"Swing your leg over her back. I'll help you up," Pierre said. Cécile got on and grabbed the harness in front of her.

Pierre tapped Bella's side two times, and slowly the elephant rose. Her trunk swayed back and forth, along with her massive body. Cécile felt as if she were on top of the world. She had never been so high in the air. Maybe this was how the circus performers felt! The elephant's step jarred her body up and down, and her heartbeat raced. She wanted to scream in fear and cry out with joy. A chilly wind brought a spatter of raindrops, but Cécile didn't even notice.

Armand shouted, "You're doing it, Cécé!

You're riding an elephant all by yourself."

Cécile grinned at her brother, lifted one hand from the harness, and gave him a tiny wave. She was so excited that she had no thought for anything except the elephant ride.

Then, a short distance beyond Armand, Cécile caught sight of two small figures. She leaned forward, squinting. Was it possible? Yes, the two cloaked children from the night before were walking along the wharf toward her and the elephant. She recognized their thin faces, slanting eyes, and flowing dark hair.

*They must have the necklace,* Cécile thought. Perhaps they had picked it up last night and were now bringing it back. She felt happiness sweep over her. This was a miracle day.

And then four things happened all at once. The sky opened up and sheets of rain began to fall. Pierre let go of the rope to grab a tarp lying nearby. A bolt of lightning streaked across the sky, followed by an earsplitting clap of thunder.

The next few moments were a blur to Cécile as Bella reared up slightly and began to trot

toward the showboat. People already racing for
shelter screamed, scrambling out of Bella's way.
The elephant crashed on, knocking over anything
in her path. Horses neighed as they bolted out of
the giant animal's way.

Cécile clutched at the harness. "Help!" she
called out. "Help!"

"Hold on tight, Cécé," Armand yelled. He
and Pierre raced alongside the elephant.

And then Cécile spotted the two children
running straight toward her and Bella. Cécile
could see now that they were a boy and a girl,
not much older than she was. She yelled to
them, "Move! Get out of the way!" But they kept
running toward her, their cloaks drenched,
their long hair clinging to their rain-splattered
faces. She called out to them again, this time in
French. Still they ran, stopping only a few feet
in front of Bella. There they stood, wide-legged,
the only thing between the elephant and the
plank leading to the circus showboat.

A scream tore from Cécile's throat. In
that second, all that mattered to her was the

children's safety. She shouted louder, demanding that they move.

They did not flinch. The boy stepped closer to Bella, talking to her, reaching his hands out to her. The elephant stood still. The boy rubbed Bella's trunk, murmuring to her.

Cécile heard someone yelling behind her, but she was too scared to turn around. Then she felt someone's hand on her leg and heard a loud command. Bella sank down on her knees. Armand and an older man of color whom Cécile hadn't seen before lifted her off. Pierre led Bella away, using the tarp to shield his face from the rain. The man gently steadied Cécile, helping her to stand.

Cécile turned to thank the two children, but they had vanished.

Armand hugged Cécile. "Are you all right?" he asked, his voice quivering.

Cécile nodded, sniffling, as the rain beat against her face.

The older man helped Cécile inside the warehouse. "Sit down," he said, patting a crate.

Cécile sat, but her legs refused to stop shaking.

"I'm so sorry, Cécé," Armand said. "I thought it would be fun."

The man patted Cécile's hand. "How did you get on that elephant, anyway?" he asked.

"I let her ride, sir," Pierre said as he stepped inside. "Sorry, sir."

"You were only supposed to walk Bella around and bring her right back," the man said sharply. "You could have gotten a lot of people hurt."

Pierre bent his head and apologized again. He hurried off to get Cécile a drink of water.

"You're both lucky that young boy was there to stop Bella," the man said. "Pierre works with the elephants, but he's too green to know that Bella doesn't like thunder."

Pierre came back only long enough to hand Cécile a tin cup. She sipped and shivered for a few minutes in silence.

Armand broke the silence. "I'm Armand Rey, and this is my sister, Cécile. Thank you for helping her."

The man shook his hand. "I'm John," he said.

"Monsieur," Cécile asked, "the boy who stopped the elephant—does he work in the circus?"

Monsieur John shook his head. "No, but sometimes he comes over and talks to the tigers and to Bella. I have seen that boy call the tigers, and they come. Even the trainer can't make them obey without a whip. The girl's his sister. They never hang around long. The cops say they're pickpockets and thieves. I don't know about that, though."

Cécile's heart sank. "Do you know where they live?" she asked.

"Not really. I think they might be orphans. They usually have those cypress baskets to sell." He shrugged. "I suspect they live in the swamps. That's where the cypress grows." He paused, glanced around, and lowered his voice. "I think they're maroons, but don't repeat that."

Cécile frowned. She knew of the cypress swamps that started at the edge of town and went on for miles. She shuddered at the thought of dark forests swarming with alligators and mosquitoes. Sensible people stayed out of the swamps.

"I'm sorry, monsieur, but what are maroons?" Cécile asked.

"Maroons are mostly runaway slaves who live in the swamps," Monsieur John explained. "I've heard they have a way with animals. What that boy did today with Bella was remarkable. Once an animal gets spooked like that, it's hard even for a trainer like me to settle her down."

Armand said, "I didn't realize there were men of color who were elephant trainers."

"Yep, I've trained elephants for many years."

Ordinarily Cécile would have been full of questions for a man who trained elephants. But right now she wanted to know more about the two children. She needed to find them to see if they had the necklace. "I want to thank those children and ask them about something," Cécile said. "Do you know how I could find them? Do they come here on certain days?"

"No, miss. They just sort of appear out of nowhere and then they're gone. I think they might

44

trade those baskets at the French Market, though. I've seen them there myself once or twice."

"Cécé," Armand said, "the rain has stopped. We should go home. Did you have any luck at the Lost and Found?"

"You lost something?" Monsieur John asked.

Before she could answer, Armand spoke up. "My sister lost her favorite blue gloves as she left the circus last night. That's why we're here."

"Did you find them, miss?" Monsieur John asked.

"No, I didn't," Cécile replied, once again wishing the gloves really were what she'd lost.

"I'll keep an eye out for your gloves, miss."

"Thank you," Cécile said, realizing that telling a fib really was a problem. Now, even if someone at the circus did have her necklace, Monsieur John couldn't help her because he'd be looking for gloves. Cécile thought of something Grand-père often said: "A lie told once multiplies like fleas on a dog."

# 5
## CLOSE CALL

As they headed home, Cécile noticed that her brother was limping.

"It's nothing. I just got a little bruise during all the commotion," Armand said. He glanced at her and added, "We'd better keep that elephant ride between us."

"I agree," Cécile said. If Maman knew she'd been on a runaway elephant, she and Armand would most definitely be in trouble. "Can we keep something else between us?" she asked.

"What is it, Cécé?"

Cécile confessed that she had lost Tante Tay's necklace.

Armand was just about to say something when a harsh voice rang out behind them. "Stop right there, boy!"

Cécile and Armand whirled around. Two rough-looking white men were striding toward them. The shorter one had a bushy beard, and the taller one bore a scar across his cheek. They looked angry, as if they'd been trapped in a hornet's nest.

The shorter man unfolded a grimy sheet of paper and thrust it into Armand's face. "It's you, ain't it, boy?" he growled.

The other man said, "What you showing him for? He can't read it."

"I beg your pardon, monsieur," Armand said.

"Oh, he can read it, all right," the short man sneered. "Says right here he can read and write. Don't it, boy?"

Armand took the paper. Cécile felt her stomach tighten as she realized that Armand's hand was trembling.

*Who are these men?* she wondered. She moved closer to Armand and read the paper:

# THE CAMEO NECKLACE

*ONE HUNDRED DOLLARS REWARD.*
*Runaway from Jefferson Parish, a negro named*
*TOM. 6 feet high, slender face. A well-looking fellow,*
*speaks well. Can read and write. Has a defective walk*
*and a large scar on left ankle. As to his clothing,*
*I cannot be certain. Likely he will endeavor to pass*
*as a freeman. Whoever delivers said slave to me shall*
*have the reward that is offered.*

Cécile's heart thumped loudly in her chest. These men were slave catchers—and they thought Armand was the man they were looking for! He had been limping because of the bruise on his leg. He was tall and handsome and spoke well. And he could read and write.

"Sir, if you'll give me a moment," Armand said, "I will show you my papers." He reached into his coat pocket for the document that proved he was a free person.

The taller man grabbed Armand's arm and twisted it behind his back. "Stop right there. You looking for a weapon, boy?"

Armand said, "I'm trying to get out my

papers, nothing else—"

"Shut your mouth," the shorter man said. "We know it's you."

Cécile's stomach twisted. In the last year or so, Papa had become more and more insistent that they carry their papers whenever they went out, and now she understood why. She felt panic rising. What if Armand had left his papers at home? "My brother doesn't have a scar on his ankle, sir!" she said.

The shorter man yanked up Armand's left trouser leg and pulled back his stocking. A fresh purple bruise had risen on his ankle, but there was no scar. "She's right," he muttered.

The taller man still did not let Armand go.

"Sir," Armand said. His voice shook, and he cleared his throat. "I am the son of Jean-Claude Rey. He is a well-known stonemason here in New Orleans. We are free people of color. If you will just let me, I will show you my papers."

"I've heard of that stonemason," the shorter man said. The other man let go of Armand's arm.

49

Armand pulled a folded paper from his pocket. "Here you are, sir."

The taller man read it and handed it back. He jabbed his finger in Armand's face. "You're lucky this time, boy."

As the slave catchers left, Cécile pressed close to her brother. Armand was never afraid of anyone, but now he was shaking as much as she was. Cécile bent her head so that Armand couldn't see the tears streaming down her face. Neither of them said a word the rest of the way home.

When Cécile and Armand arrived, tired and chilled, they were relieved to find the courtyard empty except for Hannah. She was walking toward the kitchen, but she paused when she saw them.

"Are you two all right?" she asked. She nodded toward Armand's leg. "Are you hurt?"

Cécile looked at Armand. "Nothing's wrong," she said.

"I bumped my leg," Armand added quickly.

"If you'll wait a moment, I'll get something for it," Hannah offered. "I have a salve that will soothe the pain."

Armand protested, but he sat down on a bench. Hannah hurried to her room above the kitchen and returned with a small jar that she handed to Armand. As her brother applied the salve to the angry bruise on his ankle, Cécile saw the tension in his face ease a little.

She thought about what had happened to him only minutes before and shuddered. Could the slave catchers really have taken him?

Hannah bent to a nearby shrub and broke off two flowering twigs, handing one to Cécile and one to Armand. "This might cheer you both. Smell it. It's jasmine. There is no more beautiful smell."

Armand put the jasmine to his nose and took a deep breath. He smiled. "Thank you," he said.

Cécile smelled the jasmine, but the sweet scent wasn't enough to soothe her heart. After today, she would never again feel quite so safe in New Orleans. And it didn't help that Tante Tay's necklace was still missing.

"Merci, Hannah," Cécile said. "I'm going to my room for a while."

Hannah came up with her and set out dry clothes. Then she said gently, "I wanted to show you something." She went to Cécile's dresser and opened a drawer. "I heard you telling your mother that you'd lost your blue gloves. I thought you might like to know that I found them on your bed after you left for the circus. I folded them and put them away for you."

Cécile caught her breath. This morning in the courtyard, Hannah had known that Cécile was fibbing about the gloves—but she hadn't given her away. Cécile said, "Please don't—"

Hannah broke in. "It's all right, Miss Cécile." She paused and then added quietly, "Sometimes even when we don't want to, we must keep secrets." She slipped from the room.

Cécile stared after her, surprised and grateful.

# 6
## AN UNEXPECTED INVITATION

Just before supper, Armand knocked on Cécile's door. He had changed into dry clothes, too, and Cécile noticed that his limp was better.

Armand put an arm around her shoulder. "That was quite an afternoon we had, Cécé. I wanted to be sure you're all right."

Cécile gave him a nod.

"And we didn't finish talking about Tante Tay's necklace," he added. "I'll help you if I can. Do you have any other ideas where it could be?"

Cécile had been thinking about that very thing. She told Armand she suspected that the two cloaked children had stolen it. Many people seemed to think they were thieves. And yet, somehow, both last night and today Cécile had had the strongest feeling that the children were trying to talk with her. "It hardly matters which is true. I don't know their names. I don't know where they live. How can I possibly find them?" Cécile sighed. "And then again, maybe they don't have the necklace at all."

"Who else might have it?" Armand asked.

Cécile told him about the man selling orange buns, the strange old woman, and the circus performer in her purple and gold costume. "It might even have been Agnès or Fanny Metoyer!" she said.

Armand snorted. "Cécé, the Metoyers are one of the richest families in New Orleans. Why would Agnès or Fanny steal anything?"

"You should have seen the way Agnès admired Tante Tay's necklace," Cécile replied. "She couldn't take her eyes off it. She even said it would look lovely on her."

Armand looked doubtful. "Two vagabond street children seem much more likely culprits to me." He paused. "Didn't John say he'd seen them at the French Market?"

Cécile's eyes widened. After the scare with

the slave catchers, she'd forgotten about that. "Oui, he thought they might trade their baskets there." She chewed her lip, thinking. She visited the market almost every week with Maman or Grand-père, but she had never noticed the children. She usually went later in the day, though. Perhaps the children came to trade in the early mornings, when the market was busiest.

"Tomorrow, I'll get up early and go with Mathilde," she said.

"I wish I could take you myself." Armand worked with Papa at the stone yard every day, although he had studied art in Paris and one day wanted to become a professional painter. "I hope when I come home tomorrow, you'll tell me you've gotten the necklace back, Cécé."

Downstairs, someone was knocking at the front door. They heard the sound of Maman's voice as she answered it.

A few moments later, Maman walked into Cécile's room and handed her a beautiful cream-colored envelope. Cécile saw her name scripted perfectly on the front: *Cécile A. Rey.*

# The Cameo Necklace

"Who is it from, Maman?" The only person she could think of who might send her a letter was Marie-Grace, but this was not her friend's handwriting.

"Open it," Maman said, smiling.

Cécile carefully removed the pink silk ribbon from the envelope and lifted the flap. Inside was an elegant invitation. She read it aloud:

> *We request the pleasure of your presence*
> *at a formal tea*
> *Wednesday at three o'clock.*
> *Agnès & Fanny Metoyer*

Agnès and Fanny! Cécile thought she would rather do a hundred algebra problems than spend her Wednesday afternoon at one of the Metoyer sisters' teas.

"How nice of them to invite you," Maman said. "We must get you something special to wear."

Cécile was about to say she didn't want to go but quickly changed her mind. Despite

Armand's reaction, she still thought it possible that Agnès had taken the necklace—she'd hardly been able to stop looking at it at the circus. Suddenly, Cécile recalled Agnès waving good-bye after the commotion on the wharf. Had she been holding the necklace in her other hand? Cécile held out hope; at least if Agnès had the necklace, Cécile had a chance to get it back.

Hadn't the old woman told Cécile to open her eyes? Well, Cécile's eyes were wide-open now. She saw that Agnès Metoyer could have Tante Tay's necklace. If Cécile hadn't found it by Wednesday, the tea would give her a chance to ask the Metoyers some questions. Perhaps she'd even have a chance to look for the necklace. *Yes, thank you, Agnès and Fanny.*

Of course, the truth was, the man selling orange buns could have the necklace, and so could the circus performer, the old woman, and certainly the two children. However, Cécile wouldn't be surprised at all if Agnès Metoyer had it.

Satisfied, she said to Maman, "I'm pleased

they invited me, too." She would take every opportunity she could think of to find Tante Tay's necklace. She had only five days left.

That night, Cécile lay awake while rain drummed on the roof. What if she didn't find the necklace? How could she face her aunt? Cécile tossed and turned.

Finally, listening carefully to be sure that everyone had gone to bed, she slipped into Tante Tay's room. She slid open the drawer where her aunt kept the necklace. The black velvet box was sitting where Tante Tay had left it. Cécile picked up the box, holding her breath. She squeezed her eyes shut and said a silent prayer: *Please let the necklace be in its box.* She opened the lid and looked down. The box was empty.

Tears sprang to her eyes. She had wished so hard that, for just a moment, she had thought the necklace might actually reappear. But she knew the truth—she was too old to believe in magic.

She climbed back into bed and tried to sleep. Tomorrow, she would get up early so that she could accompany Mathilde to the market. If she were lucky, she might find the two children there and come home with Tante Tay's necklace.

When Cécile awoke on Monday morning, she was glad to see that the rain had stopped and the sky was still tinted pink with dawn. Cécile was grateful to find a glass of fresh juice sitting on her nightstand. Hannah must have brought it, so quietly that Cécile hadn't even heard her come into the room.

Cécile hurried downstairs, uncovered Cochon's cage, gave him a handful of pecans, and rushed through the courtyard to the kitchen. Mathilde often went to the market before the rest of the household was stirring. Cécile breathed a sigh of relief to see her standing at the hearth, bent over a steaming kettle.

"Bonjour, Cécé," Mathilde greeted her,

smiling. "Would you like anything special from the market today? I will be going soon."

Cécile hesitated. "May I go with you?" she asked, hoping Mathilde wouldn't ask why. She didn't want to tell any more fibs, and besides, Mathilde had some mysterious way of knowing if you weren't telling the whole truth.

"Yes, you may go with me, Cécé. Go and get ready now. I will be leaving soon."

Cécile rushed upstairs to get dressed. She was about to leave her room when she thought of the two slave catchers yesterday. She remembered the look of terror on her brother's face. She opened a drawer and took out the folded paper that said Cécile Rey was a free person of color. She tucked it into her pocket. From now on, she would not set foot outside the house without it.

Back in the courtyard, Cécile was surprised to find Armand already up and seated in front of his easel, humming cheerfully. He must have decided to paint until it was time to go to the stone yard with Papa.

"Bonjour. You're in a good mood, Armand,"

Cécile said. She noticed a twig of jasmine tucked behind his ear. "What are you painting?"

"Nothing," Armand said.

Cécile smiled. "You're out here in the early-morning dew, painting nothing?"

"I'm painting flowers," Armand said.

Cécile looked at the small table where Armand usually put the real-life objects he painted. He had explained to her the importance of looking at the objects as he worked, to make sure his brushstrokes captured the way things appeared. There were no flowers on the table. Was he painting the flowers in the garden? She was about to ask when Mathilde stepped into the courtyard and called, "Are you ready, Cécile?"

Armand held a finger to his lips.

Cécile wanted to say, "You surely are acting strange," but she just hugged her brother instead. She spoke softly into his ear, "I'm off to look for those two children at the French Market."

Armand whispered back, "Good luck."

# 7

## THE FRENCH MARKET

Cécile and Mathilde walked briskly through the muddy streets. While Mathilde talked about what she was planning for their dinner and supper, Cécile tried to picture the children she would be looking for. They both had wavy black hair and complexions that reminded her of the Indians she occasionally saw in the market. She realized that she couldn't quite remember their features or recall for sure what color their cloaks were. It was almost, she thought, as if she'd dreamed them.

"Cécé," Mathilde said, "are you listening to me?"

"I'm sorry," Cécile said. She'd been so deep in thought, she hadn't even realized Mathilde was talking. How could she be so rude? "Thank you, Mathilde, for taking me with you," she said.

Mathilde turned and studied her a moment before saying, "You're welcome, Cécile."

They soon reached the market, which was even more hectic in the early morning than at midday. It rang with the sounds of people calling out descriptions of their goods. Some vendors were still setting up, moving fresh produce from their wagons to the stalls. Some were pulling up their awnings while others went about straightening their stock. Housewives, cooks, and maids inspected the merchandise, market baskets on their arms. Mathilde walked the length of the market to start her shopping at the stalls where vegetables and fruits were sold.

Cécile followed, scanning stalls and crowds in every direction as she went. Each time Mathilde stopped to look at something, Cécile darted to the nearby stalls looking for the children or their cypress baskets. If she could find the baskets, she told herself, maybe she could find the children, too. Finally Cécile spotted a marchande putting potatoes into two baskets that seemed to be about the same size and shape as the children's. She asked Mathilde, "May I go over that way a bit?"

Mathilde said, "Oui, but don't go out of my sight."

Cécile walked over to the stand. The marchande was wiping potatoes with her apron and placing them into the baskets. The baskets didn't have the indigo stripe, but they were made of cypress.

"Bonjour, madame," Cécile said. "Those are beautiful baskets."

"Merci. I like to show off my potatoes in these baskets. I'll give you a good price on potatoes today. How many pounds?"

"Actually, I was wondering where you bought the baskets. Did you by chance get them from two children?"

"No, no. I don't buy goods from children. Too many of those ruffians steal around here. I buy all my baskets from the Old Goat Man," the woman said. She pointed toward the butchers' stalls at the far end of the market. "He's down at the meat market. White hair, white beard, looks like a goat."

Cécile thanked her and turned to go. She could see Mathilde buying cucumbers nearby.

"Did you want to buy a basket?" the woman asked. "I'll sell you one of mine."

"Merci, but I am really looking for some special baskets that have an indigo stripe. Have you seen any like that?" Cécile asked.

"The Old Goat Man has them from time to time. They cost more than his other baskets," she said, shrugging. "Too rich for my blood."

Cécile's heart was beating a little faster now, but she couldn't look for the Old Goat Man until Mathilde went to the butchers' stalls. She always made the meat market her last stop.

Cécile continued to watch for the children or their baskets as Mathilde inspected vegetables and bargained with vendors. She noticed one stall with a table at the back, where white linen cloths covered lumpy shapes. Could they be baskets? Cécile waited until Mathilde was busy looking at cabbages. She scooted to the far end of the stall and slowly lifted the corner of a cloth. No baskets, only more cabbages.

Finally Mathilde headed toward the butchers' stalls. Cécile saw feathered chickens and other fowl hanging from hooks. She and Mathilde walked by gobbling turkeys and continued past the swinging heads of hogs.

The butchers, wearing white hats and soiled aprons, stood beside hanging sides of meat, calling out to customers, weighing purchases, and wrapping them up. Cécile looked down the row of stalls. At last she spotted a butcher with white hair, a pointed white beard, and a very long nose. He had to be the Old Goat Man. If she walked down to his stall, would Mathilde still be able to see her? She headed in that direction.

She managed to get to the Old Goat Man's stall without losing sight of Mathilde. The butcher carried displays of meats and sausages at the front, but farther back, Cécile saw several rows of neatly stacked baskets. Two of the baskets had the unusual indigo stripe. Cécile's heart beat faster. She waited, shifting from one foot to another, while the Old Goat Man prepared meat for three different customers.

Cécile saw Mathilde getting closer to the stall. She hoped she'd be able to talk to the Old Goat Man before Mathilde walked up.

Finally he handed a package to his last customer and turned to Cécile. "May I get you something?" he said, a grin on his face. His teeth were yellow and crooked.

Cécile glanced around. Mathilde was three stalls away. "Oui, I wanted to ask you about your baskets."

"Which ones are you interested in?" the Old Goat Man asked. He reached into the back and lifted a straw basket that had a grass-covered handle. "This is a nice one."

"I was looking at those," Cécile said, pointing to the indigo-striped baskets.

"Aww, a girl with good taste," the Old Goat Man said, chuckling. "These are my special baskets. They aren't just any old cypress baskets. They come right out of the Louisiana swamps. You won't find any quite like 'em here in the market."

"Did you get them from two children?" Cécile asked.

Suddenly the grin left the butcher's face and his eyes narrowed slightly. "Why do you ask?"

Cécile said, "I just wanted to know where you got them."

The Old Goat Man turned away and began cleaning one of his knives with a cloth. "I trade with a lot of people. Can't remember where I got the baskets."

Cécile didn't want to be impolite, but she couldn't give up yet. "Monsieur, I thought you said the baskets came right out of the swamps."

"Did I say that?" He set down his knife and cloth and turned to her. She could see that he was sweating even though the morning air was crisp and chilly. "Well, *chérie*," he said, "what of it? That's where most of the cypress trees grow."

Mathilde walked up beside Cécile, giving a friendly nod to the butcher. "Cécile, did you want some of his sausages?"

Before Cécile could answer, the Old Goat Man said, "Your girl just likes my baskets."

Mathilde looked at the neat rows of baskets. "I can see why. They're very nice."

The Old Goat Man was smiling again. "I've got tasty lamb for sale, madame."

"No, thank you," Mathilde said, handing Cécile one of the market sacks filled with vegetables to carry.

As they headed out of the market, Cécile thought about the Old Goat Man. She felt sure that he knew the children. Why wouldn't he say so? What he'd said about the baskets kept popping into her mind: *They come right out of the Louisiana swamps.* Did the two children actually live in the swamps? Cécile couldn't imagine that. Yet Monsieur John from the circus had said that some people did live there, runaway slaves he called maroons. But he had told her not to repeat that word. Cécile shivered. Were maroons dangerous? Were the two children maroons? Did this mean she would never get Tante Tay's necklace back?

Cécile was thinking about this when she smelled the scent of oranges. Then she heard a familiar voice call out, "Hot orange buns. Hot, sweet orange buns." She spun around, sniffing the air like a hound. She spotted the red-haired marchand at the edge of the market, holding his tray high. She wanted to ask him if he'd seen her necklace—but how could she talk to him without Mathilde overhearing?

Just then, Cécile had a stroke of luck. One of Mathilde's friends called to her from a vendor's cart at the edge of the market. "May I look at the baker's goods while you talk?" Cécile asked.

"Yes, but stay in sight," Mathilde replied.

Cécile waited for Mathilde to reach her friend before rushing over to the marchand. He had set down his almost-empty tray and was at his wagon now, laying out loaves of bread.

"Bonjour, monsieur," Cécile said. "May I interrupt you for a moment, please?"

The man turned, holding a loaf as if it were an extension of his arm. "You already did," he said, smiling. Then he tilted his head. "Wait—haven't I seen you before?"

"Yes, outside the *Floating Palace* on Saturday

night," Cécile said, hopeful now. "We bumped into each other on the wharf, and I fell when you spilled your tray of buns." She glanced back over her shoulder. Mathilde was still talking. "Sir, I lost my necklace when I fell."

Cécile watched for his reaction, searching his face for a sign of guilt, but the man just stood quietly, waiting for her to say more.

"I was hoping maybe you had seen it."

He shook his head.

"Are you sure?" Cécile asked, glancing over her shoulder again. "It was a cameo on black lace, with a black ribbon. It must have come off when I fell. I came back to look for it as soon as I realized it was gone. You were still there, and you were looking down at your hand. I was hoping maybe you'd picked up the necklace."

Cécile held her breath. She hoped it didn't sound as if she was accusing him.

"Oh yes, I scraped my hand on something when I gathered up the tray. Anyway, let me think," he said, putting his hand on his chin. "You know, I did see a circus performer pick up something and put it in her purse." With a chuckle he added, "I noticed because at first I thought she was putting orange buns in her purse. Then I realized she wouldn't put those sticky buns in a fancy jeweled purse. Maybe she picked up your necklace."

Mathilde walked up beside Cécile and peered at the orange buns still left on the tray. "Mmm, is that something new you have there?" she asked.

"Oui, a new recipe. Just trying it out this week. Hot orange buns."

"I'll take two," Mathilde said, winking at Cécile.

"Coming right up," he replied.

Cécile's mind was already churning. This man didn't have her necklace. She hadn't found the two children, and the one man who had their baskets wouldn't admit to knowing them.

At least the orange-bun man had given her a hopeful clue. She had to get back to the circus.

# 8
## TROUBLING QUESTIONS

After supper that evening, Cécile sat in the parlor with her family. Maman was mending one of Papa's shirts. Papa played chess with Armand while Grand-père read the newspaper and Hannah quietly tended the fire. Usually Cécile loved these quiet times with her family, but tonight she barely heard a word that anyone said. She couldn't concentrate on her embroidery stitches, either. She was too worried.

After she and Mathilde had gotten home from the market, Cécile had racked her brain for a way to get back to the *Floating Palace*. She had to follow the clue the orange-bun man had given her.

She'd decided that Grand-père was her best bet—he usually had time to spare and always enjoyed outings with her. All afternoon, she'd been trying to find a moment alone with him, but she'd had no luck. Every moment that ticked by meant that Tante Tay's return was closer.

Cécile looked down at the handkerchief she was embroidering. Its dark blue flower looked more like a spider. She sighed and pulled out her stitches again.

"What is the matter with you, Cécile?" Maman said. "You've started over on that flower twice already."

Cécile frowned. Her mother rarely sounded so cross. On his perch, Cochon gave a squawk.

"Ah, chérie, I'm sorry," Maman said, rubbing her forehead. "I have a fierce headache this evening."

"I'll make you some tea, madame," Hannah said.

When Hannah returned, Maman took a sip of the tea and looked up. "I don't believe I've had this tea before, have I?"

"I made it with herbs to ease your headache, madame. It should help you sleep, too."

Maman sipped the tea. Hannah leaned

toward Cécile and said, "If you would like, I'll show you a beautiful stitch you might use."

Cécile said "Merci" and held out the handkerchief.

Hannah sat down beside Cécile, taking the needle gently between her fingers. "See, bring the needle up here, loop the thread around, and bring the needle down here."

Cécile watched her delicate fingers expertly pulling the needle through the cloth.

Maman said, "That's a lovely stitch. Did your mother teach you that?"

"I don't remember who taught me this one, madame," Hannah replied. She passed the handkerchief back to Cécile. "Do you think you can finish it?"

Cécile nodded. Hannah hurried to stoke the fireplace, and then she picked up a broom and began sweeping the hearth.

"Hannah, you have already worked longer than necessary today," Maman said. "Take your leave now. We'll see you in the morning."

"Oui, madame." Hannah curtsied. "Are you

sure there's nothing else you need?"

"My head feels better already," Maman said. "And I'm sure if any of us needs anything, we can manage. Go and get some rest."

Armand looked up from his game. "Good night, Hannah." Cécile saw Maman cut a glance at Papa.

"Good night, everyone." Hannah curtsied again and quickly slipped from the room.

Shortly, Maman announced that she was going to bed. Papa and Armand packed up their game, and Grand-père yawned and folded his newspaper. Cécile covered Cochon's cage and went upstairs, still worrying about how she would get back to the *Floating Palace*.

She was almost ready to crawl into bed when she noticed a flickering light out her window. She stepped out on the balcony. In the courtyard below, Armand was sitting at his easel. He was painting in the chill night by the flickering light of several lamps and candles.

Cécile frowned. Armand never painted at night.

Cécile threw on her shawl and tiptoed down to join him, trying hard to be quiet so that no one else would hear and come out. She wanted to talk to Armand alone. She still hadn't told him about her morning at the market.

Cécile flinched as she felt the crunch of a rock under her slipper. "Ouch!" she murmured.

Armand quickly threw a cloth over his painting.

"You don't have to do that," Cécile said quietly. "It's just me."

"I'm not ready to show anyone yet," Armand said, wiping off his brushes with a damp rag. "I may show it to you when I'm finished."

Cécile thought he was teasing. He had always let her see his work. "I'd love to see it now," she said with a smile, lifting the cloth before Armand could stop her.

Cécile stared at the painting. It was only half finished, but she could see it was a portrait of an elegant young lady, richly dressed. Already she could tell it would be lovely. "You are such a fine painter, Armand," she whispered. The partially completed face looked vaguely familiar. Was it a woman she'd seen at church, or at the opera or a ball? "Armand," Cécile said excitedly, "you haven't gotten a commission to paint a portrait, have you?" Being paid to do a painting was what her brother had been hoping for. It would be a step toward reaching his dream.

Armand shook his head. He grabbed the cloth from Cécile and put it back over the painting. "I didn't plan to show it to anyone."

"Why not?" Cécile asked. "It's beautiful."

Armand fidgeted with his brushes, looking at the ground. Cécile saw a look in her brother's face that she'd never seen before.

"You wouldn't understand," he said. Then he patted her shoulder. "Now tell me, what happened at the market? Did you find the necklace?"

Cécile quickly filled him in. "I'll ask Grandpère to take me to the *Floating Palace* tomorrow," she concluded.

"When you get there," Armand suggested, "look for John or Pierre. They'll know how to

find the performer." He wished her luck and
shooed her off to bed.

In the middle of the night, Cécile woke up.
She had been dreaming that she was explaining
to Tante Tay about the necklace, when suddenly
her aunt put her hands to her face and began
to sob as if her heart would break. As Cécile
awoke, she realized that her own face was wet
with tears.

She sat up in bed, her throat tight. The dream
had seemed so real. She would go back to the
*Floating Palace* tomorrow, but what if the circus
performer didn't have the necklace? Where else
could she look?

Cécile thought about all the other people
who might have it. She no longer suspected
the orange-bun seller, and she would go to the
Metoyers' house on Saturday. What about the
old woman who had said such strange things
to her? Cécile's arms felt as if tiny fireflies had

lit upon them. She wondered if the woman was crazy. Would that make her more or less likely to be a thief? Cécile didn't know. It didn't matter, since she had no idea how to find the old woman anyway.

Her mind went back to the two children. Twice, she'd had the feeling they were coming to talk to her. She had to keep looking for them. Where else could she search?

Monsieur John had mentioned one more detail—that the police thought the children might be orphans. Cécile considered that. Ever since the yellow fever epidemic last year, she had volunteered often at Children of Mercy Orphanage. It was the only orphanage in the city for children of color. If the two children lived there, Cécile would have noticed them. She was sure of that.

Of course, everyone knew that there were many orphans who refused to live in orphanages. They slept in the alleys of the poorest neighborhoods, and the police always chased them because they stole from the shops and marchands. Some of them were pickpockets. If the two children lived like that, it would explain why they were chased off the wharf on Saturday night. But how could she find two orphans living on the worst streets of the city?

Or maybe they didn't live on the streets, but, as Monsieur John suspected, in the swamps. If they did live in the swamps, she knew she might never find them.

Cécile felt her frustration growing. Suddenly another feeling washed over her as well. Here she lay in her soft bed. Even the orphans at Children of Mercy had cots to sleep in and pillows to lay their heads on, she thought. Where did children sleep who lived in dark alleys? Or, even worse, in the swamps?

For some reason, the old woman she'd met on the wharf floated back into her mind. What had she said? Something so strange, about hunters and lions... Cécile fell asleep trying to remember the old woman's exact words.

# 9
## HUNTERS AND LIONS

Right after breakfast, Cécile found Grand-père alone in the parlor, reading the *Picayune*. He read newspapers every day. He always said he loved two things: knowing about the world and understanding what was in it.

The date on the newspaper's banner reminded Cécile that Tante Tay's return was only three days away. "Grand-père, are you busy today?" she asked.

Grand-père snapped his newspaper shut. "Yes, *ma chérie.* Why?"

Cécile's heart dropped. "I wanted to ask you to take me someplace. I suppose it can wait." It couldn't wait, really, but what else could she say?

"What I'm busy doing, ma chérie, is

whatever you want me to do." Grand-père patted her shoulder.

"Will you take me to the *Floating Palace* to talk to a man Armand and I met there?"

"Of course! I am always interested in the circus." Grand-père waved a hand at her. "What are you standing there for? Go and get ready."

A few minutes later, they were out in the bright morning sunshine. As they strolled along, Cécile told Grand-père about her scary but exciting elephant ride. She figured she had better tell him, since Monsieur John would probably mention it. Just as she had hoped, Grand-père loved the story.

"What an adventure, Cécé!" he said. "You are a brave young lady."

Cécile grinned, pleased at his reaction. Then she thought of the two children who had calmed the elephant.

"Grand-père," she asked, "have you ever heard of maroons?"

"Yes, I have." His eyes narrowed and his tone grew serious. "Who mentioned them to you?"

"The man at the circus. Do you know much about them?"

"I don't think anyone knows much about maroons," Grand-père replied. "I am surprised anyone in New Orleans was talking to you about them. That subject isn't spoken of, especially among free people of color."

"What do you mean?" Cécile asked, remembering Monsieur John telling her not to repeat the word. She thought of how the Old Goat Man had suddenly stopped acting friendly when she asked about the children.

"Let me tell you a story," Grand-père said. "Some years ago, there was a maroon named Bras-Coupé."

"That's a strange name," Cécile said.

"Well, his real name was Squire, but people called him Bras-Coupé after he lost an arm."

"Because it means 'Arm Cut Off,'" Cécile said.

"Yes. Bras-Coupé was a slave who escaped into the swamps. He became a leader of the maroons around here. People said he knew all kinds of magic—that when white men shot at him, the bullets would flatten out, and that when anyone pursued him, fog would swirl up around him and he'd just slip away, laughing. Soldiers who chased him said he'd mastered the art of camouflage."

"I know what that means," Cécile said, grateful for Monsieur Lejeune's tutoring. "It's the art of hiding in plain sight."

"Very good, Cécile. Slave owners hated Bras-Coupé. They thought he would encourage slaves to join him, enough to rise up and revolt against slavery. The state offered a reward for his death. After he was killed, soldiers left his body in the square here, in the sweltering heat of summer. For three days, they forced slaves, thousands of them, to walk past his body as a warning that they could not escape slavery." Grand-père paused. "While he lived in the swamps, Bras-Coupé was one of the most hated men in Louisiana."

"*Was* he a bad man?" Cécile asked, not sure what to think about the story.

"It depends whom you ask, chérie. Many people, even free people of color, say that he and his followers were thieves, murderers, even conjurers. But the slaves consider Bras-Coupé a hero. They sing songs about him to this very day. To them, he was a fighter for freedom."

"What do you think, Grand-père?"

"I believe that slavery is the evil, Cécé, not fighting against it. But many disagree with me, even many free people of color." Grand-père put a hand on her shoulder. "Best you don't mention maroons anymore. Too many around here don't want people to even think about being free. I hope one day for you, granddaughter, things will change."

Cécile didn't understand. Weren't she and her family free already?

A moment later, she could almost hear the two slave catchers threatening Armand. Maybe she did understand.

A steamboat whistle pierced the air. Cécile looked up. She had been listening so intently, she hadn't realized that they'd already reached the levee. Up ahead, she could see the *Floating Palace*, its flags snapping smartly in the breeze.

Cécile found Monsieur John in one of the warehouses near the *Floating Palace*, working with the elephant.

She quickly realized that no one could have enjoyed a visit to the circus more than Grand-père. He and Monsieur John hit it off at once. Monsieur John would tell a circus story, and then Grand-père would tell a story from his sailing days.

Cécile thought maybe she could find the blonde circus performer without Monsieur John's help. She excused herself and left the warehouse. She surveyed the wharf in front of the huge floating showboat. She saw crews of men piling barrels onto wagons, others stacking bales of hay, and still others standing in small groups, talking.

Then she noticed two policemen looking inside and around barrels only feet from where she stood. Cécile stopped in her tracks. What were they doing?

"I think they're still here somewhere," one policeman yelled to the other. "Keep looking!"

Cécile heard a rustling sound behind her. She turned and found herself staring at the backs of two dark-haired children, huddled behind a stack of burlap sacks piled in a corner. She recognized their tattered cloaks and the indigo-striped baskets they held by their sides.

Cécile knew that if the policemen got any closer, they would see the children. Backed into the corner, they had nowhere to run. What should she do? This might be her only chance to find out if the children had the necklace. But if she stopped to talk to them, the police would surely catch them. She remembered them standing in front of the elephant, saving her.

She glanced one last time at the children. Cécile made a decision.

She began walking toward the two policemen, thinking about her next move. How could she stop them from catching the children? She spotted a large metal bolt lying on the ground. She waited for the moment when the policemen looked into another set of barrels before throwing the bolt with all her power over the heads of both policemen into a corner of the warehouse wall behind them. She held her breath as the policemen quickly turned toward the sound they had heard and took off running.

Cécile waited, not daring to take a breath until both policemen had gone out of sight.

Cécile returned to the corner where the children had been hiding, but they were no longer there. She fought back tears, knowing that she might have lost her only chance to talk to them. But she couldn't have just stood by and let them be caught, not even if it meant that she would never get Tante Tay's necklace back. The words of the old woman floated into her mind: *Hunters always want to kill lions... Lions only want to eat.*

# 10
## MISS MILLIE

Cécile turned from the abandoned hiding place and tried to calm down. Maybe it didn't matter that she had lost her chance to talk to the children. After all, she was here because the orange-bun man had seen the blonde circus performer pick something up from the wharf. It might very well have been Tante Tay's necklace.

Cécile straightened her shoulders. She must look for the circus performer, just as she'd planned.

But Cécile didn't see any circus performers as she surveyed the *Floating Palace*. She went closer. The gangplank was down, but no sounds were coming from inside the boat.

Cécile looked back over the wharf. The doors of the nearby warehouse buildings were flung open, and people were bustling in and out. She realized that she'd been looking at the circus people all along. They just weren't wearing their costumes now.

Excitedly, she hurried back toward the warehouses, sure she'd recognize the woman with the blonde ringlets even if she wasn't in costume. Peeking into one doorway, Cécile saw men tugging on long pulleys; they must be working on the high-wire act. Through another doorway, she glimpsed a few women dressed in strange, ballooning pants, but they all had jet-black hair.

Cécile looked down the long row of warehouses and sighed. It would take too long to search them all. She'd better ask Monsieur John, even if she had to interrupt.

Monsieur John was happy to help. "I know everyone in the circus," he said.

Relieved, Cécile quickly described the woman's blonde ringlets and her gold and purple costume.

"Did she carry a fancy drawstring bag?" Monsieur John asked.

Cécile nodded hopefully. "Yes, it had a lot of jewels on it."

"That's Millie Sawell, all right. She's part of the dog act." Cécile remembered the little dogs doing flips and jumping through hoops. "Miss Millie carries that bag everywhere, even when she's no call to need it."

"What do you mean? It's her purse, isn't it?"

"Nope. It's full of treats for the dogs. They get rewards when they do their tricks right." Monsieur John leaned out the warehouse door and pointed. "Fifth building down. You'll find Miss Millie there, training the dogs."

"I'll take you, chérie," Grand-père said. He shook Monsieur John's hand. "It was my pleasure."

"Hope to see you again, mate," Monsieur John said, giving Grand-père a salute.

Cécile wondered how she would ask Miss Millie about the necklace without Grand-père hearing, but it wasn't a problem at all. Once he was inside the warehouse, the dogs raced over to Grand-père as if he were holding out a bone for them. In seconds, he was down on the floor, rubbing the dogs and talking to them as if they were old friends.

Two men came over to Grand-père, and Miss Millie followed. She wasn't wearing her shiny costume, but her blonde ringlets looked just as Cécile remembered. She held the jeweled bag in her hand.

As Grand-père and the men began talking, Cécile introduced herself to Miss Millie.

"What a lovely name," Miss Millie said. "You look familiar."

"I came to the circus Saturday night. On the wharf afterward, I stumbled and knocked a woman down. You asked me if I was all right."

"Oh my, yes. I knew I'd seen you before. You're the little one who was showered with buns. I was relieved you weren't hurt in the crowd. You could easily have been trampled. Crowds can be frightening. I admit, I like to get in the midst of the crowd, though. During the show, everyone is so far away." Miss Millie fiddled with her drawstring bag. "It's rare that

I get to see people from the audience up close. I've been in the circus all my life."

Cécile smiled, realizing that to Miss Millie, people who weren't in the circus seemed just as strange and exotic as circus performers seemed to Cécile.

"I lost my necklace when I fell," Cécile said. "Did you by chance see it?" The minute the words were out, she felt sure that Miss Millie would look at her as blankly as the orange-bun seller had.

"Was it a cameo necklace?" Miss Millie asked.

Cécile's eyes widened, and her heart skipped a beat. "Yes. Yes, it was. Do you know what happened to it? The necklace is very important to me."

"My dear, I did see it on the ground. In fact, I almost stepped on it, but someone picked it up. I'm so sorry, my dear little friend, I don't have your necklace."

Finding it hard to speak, yet still hoping, Cécile asked, "Did you see who picked it up?"

"Sorry, my dear, there was so much going on. And it was dark. I saw two hands reaching for the necklace. I do remember that. One hand had a ring on every finger. The other?" She shrugged. "I was so fascinated by all the rings, I didn't really notice. And then I had the bright idea to pick up the buns. I knew my doggies would love those for treats, and they did."

So, the orange-bun seller had been right, Cécile thought; Miss Millie had been stuffing buns into her purse.

Miss Millie patted Cécile's shoulder. "Don't be so sad, my dear. I'm sure you will find it."

Cécile thanked her and returned to Grand-père, her mind racing as she waited for him to finish his story.

The hand with a ring on every finger—it must have been the strange old woman's. Cécile could almost hear her saying, "You have lost something very valuable." Of course—how could the woman have known that unless *she'd* taken the necklace? Why hadn't Cécile realized this before now? Tears sprang to her eyes as she thought about how close she might have been to the necklace on Saturday night when the old woman grabbed her hands. Then, like a dark cloud overshadowing the sun, Cécile realized that even if by some miracle she located the old woman, that didn't mean the woman would give the necklace back. Worse, Cécile had no idea if the old woman actually had picked up the necklace. Miss Millie had said somone else reached for it, too. So the two children might have it—and Cécile had just let them get away. The only thing Cécile knew for sure was that she was no closer to finding the necklace than she'd been yesterday.

Grand-père suggested they take a carriage home. As they rode along the crowded street, Cécile felt tears slowly slinking down her face, and a salty taste rimmed her lips. She turned her head and peered out the window. She pulled out a handkerchief and wiped her tears away.

Cécile could feel Grand-père watching her, but he didn't say a word.

Cécile wished she could tell him everything.

But she didn't want to burden anyone else with her secret. Poor Hannah was already keeping her secret. Maman had often said that keeping a secret was a heavy load to bear. Cécile understood that now. She vowed that losing the necklace would be the last secret she kept.

As the carriage pulled up in front of the Reys' home, Cécile reminded herself that it was still possible Agnès Metoyer had the necklace. Cécile couldn't remember if Agnès wore a lot of rings or not. Maybe, just maybe, she did.

Tomorrow Cécile would find out once and for all if Agnès was as mean as Cécile thought she was.

# 11

## AGNÈS'S SURPRISE

The next morning, Cécile stood in front of her mirror in her party dress, watching as Maman tied a matching bow in her hair.

"Maman," Cécile said, "my hair doesn't look right."

Maman adjusted the bow.

"I don't think it's the ribbon, Maman," Cécile said. "My curls are too loose."

Hannah stopped folding Cécile's nightgown. "Madame, if you would like, I can fix her hair."

"Please, Maman, let Hannah try."

"Would you, Hannah?" Maman asked, looking relieved.

"I have a pomade that will put a nice shine in her hair and help it curl," Hannah said. "I'll get it."

A few minutes later, Hannah returned with a decorated jar. When she removed the lid, a wonderful aroma filled the room.

Cécile sat down so that Hannah could work. She felt Hannah's fingers removing the ribbon and then gently applying pomade, arranging curls, and slipping in hairpins here and there.

"You're doing a fine job, Hannah," Maman said. "Did your mother teach you?"

"No, madame," Hannah replied softly. "Cécile is a lucky girl to have her mother here to teach and help her."

Cécile could hear the sadness in Hannah's voice. She wondered if Hannah had ever known her own mother. Cécile knew that many children lost their mothers at an early age; she had learned that at the orphanage. Sitting here as Hannah arranged her hair, Cécile felt close to her. She hoped that Hannah knew she was as much a part of the family as Mathilde was.

When Hannah finished, Maman said, "My goodness, that's lovely. Merci, Hannah."

Hannah led Cécile to the mirror. "What do

you think, Miss Cécile?"

Cécile was almost afraid to look. When she did, she saw that Hannah had swept her hair up on her head in a style she'd never worn before.

Cécile took one look and hugged Hannah. "I look so grown-up! Oh, thank you, Hannah."

With a pleased smile, Hannah nodded and quietly left the room.

"Turn around, Cécile," Maman said. "Let me see you."

Cécile made a slow circle in front of the mirror, letting Maman inspect her hair and dress before she left for the Metoyers' party. As anxious as Cécile was about the necklace, she couldn't help feeling proud of the image she saw in the mirror. Her new dress was lacy and white, with small pink flowers at the neck and waist that looked almost real. Maman had even found white lace gloves with little pink flowers at the wrist. And now her hair was elegant, too.

"You look lovely, chérie," Maman said with tears in her eyes.

"What is it? Why are you crying, Maman?"

Cécile ran to her mother and hugged her close.

"My little girl is growing up, that's all," Maman said, laughing now. "Mothers want their children to grow up, and they don't want them to grow up."

Cécile understood. There was a part of her that wanted to grow up, but there was also a part of her that didn't. Instead of the world getting clearer as she got older, everything seemed to get more confusing.

Maman kissed Cécile's cheek. "Let's go downstairs. Hannah will walk you to the Metoyers'."

Butterflies danced in Cécile's stomach at the thought of Agnès and Fanny and the necklace. For some reason, the old woman's words rang in her mind: *Those you do not know have it*. Well, Cécile knew Agnès and Fanny, but sometimes she surely wished she didn't.

"Wear your warm coat," Maman said. "It's chilly out today."

Hannah was certainly dressed for cold weather, Cécile thought. She stood by the door wearing a bulky coat, a scarf on her head, and a shawl over both. Cécile smiled, thinking that Hannah was so bundled up, she looked more like Mathilde than the slender young woman she was.

Outside, they walked in silence. Hannah was always quiet, and today Cécile was too nervous to carry on any chatter. She had to make the most of this chance to find Tante Tay's necklace. She had made no progress looking for the two children. She and Armand had gone to Jackson Square last evening to search. They'd seen many marchands there, but no children offering baskets. For a moment last night, Cécile's hopes had risen as she'd glimpsed some indigo-striped baskets among one marchand's wares. But when she asked where he'd gotten them, he'd said, "From the Old Goat Man down at the French Market."

Cécile pushed the memory away. She looked at Hannah, walking with her head bent and her shawl pulled forward so that it almost hid her face. Cécile realized with some embarrassment that she'd been so busy thinking about the necklace, she hadn't said a word to Hannah yet. She thought of a question she'd been meaning to ask ever since last Sunday.

"Hannah, tell me how you know my tutor, Monsieur Lejeune. He's such a nice man and so very smart, don't you think?"

To Cécile's surprise, Hannah replied, "Monsieur Lejeune? I'm afraid I don't know anyone by that name."

"But I'm sure—" Cécile began, ready to explain that she'd seen the two of them talking in Jackson Square. But then she recalled how Hannah had kept Cécile's secret about the gloves, never asking a single question.

"I'm sorry, Hannah, I must be mistaken," Cécile said gently. "Goodness, it's cold for November, isn't it?"

Still, she couldn't help being curious about Hannah's secret. She didn't have long to ponder, though, because in the next moment what Cécile saw almost made her heart stop beating.

A white man was pulling a slave down a shadowy alley. The slave had an iron collar around his neck. His clothes were torn and his head was bowed. Cécile knew the white man was a slave catcher.

Cécile turned her head away. Her body felt numb as she remembered the two slave catchers who had stopped Armand. What if they'd taken her brother away? That man with irons around his neck could have been Armand. Cécile patted her coat pocket, feeling for the folded paper inside. There it was, but she still felt shaken. Cécile wondered how long it would be before the sight of a slave catcher didn't turn her stomach to jelly. Then she thought of the slave now being pulled along in his iron collar. She thought about his terrified face and wondered if he was someone's brother, too. She said a silent prayer for him.

Unsettled, she reached for Hannah's hand, but no one was there.

Fear gripped Cécile. Had Hannah left her all alone? She looked down the street. Hannah was only a short distance behind and was hurrying to catch up with her.

"I'm sorry, Miss Cécile," Hannah said. "I—I

thought I saw a friend across the street, but it was someone else."

"It's all right," Cécile said, glad to have Hannah beside her again.

Cécile realized that they were nearing the Metoyers' house. She had to figure out how to get Tante Tay's necklace back. What if Agnès denied having it? Then what?

The Metoyers' fancy house came into view. Cécile took a deep breath to steel her nerves. She had to be ready to confront Agnès and Fanny.

A well-dressed servant opened the Metoyers' door. She curtsied to Cécile, never glancing at Hannah.

"Welcome, mademoiselle," the servant said, motioning Cécile to follow. Cécile stepped into the house, taking one more deep breath.

"Have fun," Hannah said, speaking softly.

Cécile turned and gave her a wave, smiling.

"Thank you, Hannah," she said, patting her hair. "Merci."

Hannah smiled back.

The servant shut the door, leaving Hannah standing on the Metoyers' porch. *How rude,* Cécile thought. Then she realized that not so long ago, she would have hardly noticed.

Forcing her thoughts back to the necklace, Cécile followed the maid down a wide hallway. Red draperies with gold embroidery framed the windows, and ornate gas lamps hung on the walls. A side table held fresh flowers in silver vases. Down the hallway, Cécile heard girls' voices and laughter.

In the parlor, maids dressed in gray with white aprons were serving treats on silver trays. An older free person of color whom Cécile recognized from the cathedral sat in one corner playing a harp. The tables were set with fine china. The white tablecloths and napkins were crisply starched. Beautiful white and blue flowers had been placed in the center of each table in a blue vase.

Fanny came over to greet Cécile, looking very stylish in a blue and white silk dress. Agnès didn't seem to be in the room yet, but the other guests clustered around Cécile, admiring her hair and dress.

Cécile tried to join in the polite talk and laughter, as if her heart weren't beating double time. How would she find a chance to talk privately with Fanny and Agnès? Hoping no one would notice, Cécile cast her eyes around the room, considering whether there was any way she might later be able to slip off and find Agnès's room, to see if the necklace was there.

Madame Metoyer walked in and greeted all the girls. "We welcome you to our home," she said, waving her hand toward the buffet table. "Please enjoy the watercress sandwiches, the scones, the cookies, the teacakes, and, of course, the teas. We have three kinds. There is plenty of everything. Enjoy." With an elegant swish, she left the room.

Cécile wondered if she would be able to swallow a single bite of the delicious-looking treats. Her stomach felt as if it were full of angry bees. She had a feeling that it was going to be much harder than she had ever imagined to find out whether the Metoyers had her necklace.

At that moment, Agnès waltzed into the room as if she were dancing on clouds, smiling and greeting everyone. She looked elegant in a blue silk dress with a matching ribbon in her hair and—

Cécile gasped. There it was, right before her eyes—the cameo necklace. *Agnès was wearing the cameo necklace.*

Cécile felt as if someone had thrown hot pepper in her face. How could Agnès steal her necklace and then flaunt it right in front of her?

A swarm of girls surrounded Agnès. One girl said, "I love the black lace under the cameo." Another said, "Yes, it makes it look so fancy. I've never seen a cameo on black lace before."

Cécile could not stop herself. She pushed her way through the guests until she was face-to-face with Agnès. "How could you?" Cécile said. She could not hold back. "How could you do this?"

"Are you upset?" Agnès asked, frowning.

"Why, I thought you would be flattered."

*Flattered?* Cécile was so angry, she couldn't even answer.

Fanny rushed over. "Oh dear, Cécile. I told Agnès you might not be pleased."

Agnès shrugged and spoke to her sister as if they were the only two there. "I already told Cécile how very pretty I thought her necklace was. Why should she care if I had Rudine sew black lace under my cameo, too?"

Cécile stared at the necklace. Now she saw that it wasn't Tante Tay's ivory cameo at all. The fine profile was carved from a pinkish stone. With a pang of shame, she realized that Agnès might not even have seen Cécile's necklace on the wharf.

Cécile looked up to see all the girls staring at her as if she were a pirate who had just landed with a stolen ship. "I—I'm sorry, Agnès," she managed.

Fanny touched her arm. "I did tell Agnès you might not like her copying your necklace."

"Cécile, honestly, I wasn't trying to make

you feel bad," Agnès added. "I think your necklace is the prettiest cameo I've ever seen. Why, you should be proud that you've started a new fashion."

Cécile tried to smile, but she couldn't meet Agnès's eyes. This time, she knew, *she* was the one who had behaved badly.

Cécile let Fanny lead her to the buffet table. The other girls began to chatter, and the party resumed. Cécile somehow got through the rest of the tea, but her mind was as jumbled as a jigsaw puzzle.

When the party ended, Cécile was relieved to find Armand waiting for her in the Metoyers' entryway. On the way home, she told him how she had embarrassed herself.

"Well," Armand said, "at least you know the Metoyers don't have the necklace."

"But that leaves only the two children and the old woman—and I can't find them. And

Tante Tay will be home in two days." The tears that had been threatening all through the party finally spilled over.

Armand put his arm around his sister. "Cécé, I've been thinking. There's one more place we haven't looked. After you get out of that party dress, we'll go to Congo Square."

Cécile caught her breath. Congo Square was where the slaves and poorer free people of color gathered to visit, dance, and trade. It was shabbier than Jackson Square, with bare dirt instead of green lawns. Sometimes soldiers practiced marching there. Cécile had not been to Congo Square very often, but she knew that some marchands sold treats and trinkets there.

"That's a good idea, Armand. Merci," said Cécile, walking faster now. There was no time to lose. Tante Tay would be home the day after tomorrow.

# 12
## MESSAGE IN CONGO SQUARE

"Rice cakes! Hot, fresh rice cakes!"

"Good price on beads. Come, take a look!"

In the dusty square at the edge of the French Quarter, marchands sat with their wares spread out on blankets, urging passersby to make a purchase. Cécile and Armand walked past them slowly, asking the marchands if they had any indigo-striped baskets for sale. They went from one end of the square to the other and then decided to split up and try again.

Cécile was on the verge of giving up when she saw a figure sitting near a tree on a make-shift chair. It seemed to be an old woman wearing a colorful tignon on her head and strings of beads around her neck. Cécile caught her breath. Was it the old woman from the wharf? Cécile was too far away to be sure.

She looked for Armand, but he was on the far side of the square, talking to a friend.

Cécile turned back toward the woman. Two sailors were talking with her now. Keeping to the edge of the square, where there were more trees, Cécile moved closer, her heart pounding.

Yes, she was sure now that this was the old woman she'd stumbled into on the wharf. Cécile remembered the old woman's hand moving in front of her face, with rings on every finger. She could hear the old woman's words: *You have lost something valuable.* Did she have the necklace?

As Cécile watched, the two sailors left, and a well-dressed young lady walked up to the old woman. Cécile could see them talking, but she couldn't hear what they were saying. She had to get closer.

Staying in the shadows of the trees, Cécile inched closer. She still couldn't hear, but she could see better now. The young lady handed money to the old woman, but the old woman didn't seem to give her anything in return.

A line was forming in front of the old woman. As the young lady left, a man wearing a top hat stepped forward. Cécile watched carefully. Again, the old woman received money but seemed to give nothing in return. Cécile was puzzled. Was the old woman a pickpocket who came to Congo Square to sell items she had stolen? Was she cleverly keeping the stolen items hidden as she passed them over to the buyers?

Cécile felt sure that Armand would know what was happening. She didn't want to leave the cover of the trees, but she hoped he'd come this way soon. She could see him looking around for her now. She waved to him. Armand didn't see her.

Cécile looked back at the old woman. The man in the top hat had gone, and a well-dressed free person of color who attended Cécile's church was talking with the old woman. Once again, the old woman accepted money but seemed to give nothing in return. Cécile waited until the next person in line was talking with the old woman, and then she ran to catch up with the lady from her church.

"Bonjour, madame," Cécile said. "May I ask a question of you, please?"

"Oui, ma chérie," she said. "You are the Reys' daughter, am I correct?"

"Oui, madame. I was wondering what the woman under that tree is selling."

"Dreams," replied the lady.

Cécile felt confused. *Dreams?* How could anyone sell dreams?

"What I mean is, she's a seer," the lady explained. "God has given Madame Irène the gift of sight."

"What is the gift of sight?" Cécile asked. The old woman's voice echoed in her mind: *Open your eyes so you can see.*

"She knows things, my dear. Sometimes she simply knows how you feel or what you want, and sometimes she can see what is going to happen in the future."

Cécile stood dumbfounded for a few seconds before murmuring, "Merci."

Cécile looked over at the old woman. She

was standing up now, gathering her things. Cécile's breath caught in her throat. *Oh no,* she thought. If she didn't move quickly, she would lose any chance to talk to the old woman. Did Cécile dare ask her for the necklace?

Cécile scanned the square. She glimpsed Armand walking in the opposite direction, looking around for her.

The old woman was already walking away. Cécile ran to catch her without thinking what she would say. If the old woman wanted money, Cécile would borrow it from Armand. Time was running out.

A small throng of people leaving the square blocked Cécile's view of the woman, and she thought she'd lost her. Then she heard someone calling her name. It wasn't Armand's voice.

"Come, Cécile," the old woman called to her. "I knew you would be here today."

Cécile thought, *It's easy for her to say that she knew I'd come, since I'm already here—but how does she know my name?*

The old woman stepped closer. Cécile could

see the wisps of gray hair that had escaped from her tignon, and the deep wrinkles in her weathered face. "Don't be afraid, ma chérie," the old woman said.

Cécile stared at her, unable to speak.

"Go on. You might as well ask me," the old woman said. "My name is Madame Irène, by the way. Go on. Don't be shy."

Cécile knew that the old woman was right; she had to ask, no matter how terrified she felt. She heard Grand-père's voice telling her how brave she was.

She swallowed and cleared her throat. Finally, the words came out. "Madame, do you have my necklace?"

Madame Irène's dark eyes looked into Cécile's. "*Your* necklace? Are you sure about that?"

Cécile stepped back in terror. How did the old woman know the necklace wasn't hers? Cécile's fear increased, but she pressed on. "I lost my necklace on the wharf. I was hoping that you had it. One of the circus performers said she saw someone with a ring on each finger pick it up." Cécile's eyes moved to Madame Irène's hands. There were rings on every finger.

Madame Irène smiled. "So you didn't think I'd stolen it?"

Cécile felt the same heat she had felt the night they'd met. Perspiration trickled down her forehead. The heat seemed unbearable, even though Cécile felt as if the air in her lungs had turned to icy water.

Cécile whispered, "I didn't say you stole it."

"I told you, little one: Those we cannot know have your necklace." The old woman closed her eyes. "Daughter of Aurélia...beautiful woman. Strong."

*Aurélia?*

"How do you know my mother's name?" Cécile asked. "Is this some kind of trick?" Her thoughts felt fuzzy, as if she had been standing too long in the heat of the summer sun.

Madame Irène smiled. "My dear, I know many things without being told."

The old woman went on slowly. "Cécile, you

are a very good girl; I have seen your heart. You will find what you seek." Her gnarled fingers brushed Cécile's hand.

Cécile snatched her hand away.

"Open your eyes as I told you, and you will find something even more valuable than the necklace."

Cécile's thoughts swam. The old woman had said almost the same thing on the wharf. *Open your eyes so you can see.*

Cécile shook her head, trying to clear the confusion from her mind.

"It will be all right," Madame Irène said. "Everyone makes mistakes. If it helps you to know, you will get the necklace back soon. Very soon. And you will learn much more than you seek."

Once again, the woman touched Cécile's hand. "Open your eyes, Cécile Rey."

# 13
## CHASE

"Cécile! Cécé!" Armand called. The old woman had already walked away, disappearing into the crowd.

Cécile turned to see her brother trotting toward her across the square. She watched as he suddenly slowed and waved to a friend. Armand called to Cécile, "Wait right there."

Cécile sat down on a bench, thinking about all the troubles she'd had in the last week. She felt overwhelmed. She was trying to think of what she could possibly say to Tante Tay, when she looked up and saw the two children once again walking toward her, their jet-black hair flowing as they moved.

Hardly able to believe what she was seeing, Cécile watched the two children walk toward her. In their dark cloaks, they looked almost like twins, except that the girl had beads in her hair. The dust around them seemed to glow as the last rays of the sun lit their faces. Their clothes were ragged, yet Cécile thought there was something regal about both of them.

She sat very still, waiting for them. They were only a few yards away when Cécile saw the girl reach into her cloak and then hold out something in her hand. Could it be the necklace? The old woman had said she would get it back. The girl waved to her, and Cécile dared to hope that her prayers were being answered.

Then she saw a blur of motion and heard pounding footsteps. In a flash, the children turned and took off running in the other direction.

Cécile yelled, "Wait! Wait!"

It was too late. Two policemen thundered past. The children ran away as quickly as deer in a forest. Cécile raced after them, calling back to Armand, "Come on! It's them!"

She heard Armand shouting for her to stop,

but she kept running after the policemen and the children, out of Congo Square and into the neighborhood beyond. Cécile didn't take her eyes from the four figures racing ahead.

After several blocks, the policemen stopped their chase. They doubled over, panting like dogs, and then turned down a side street, shaking their heads. Beyond them, the children kept on running, never looking back.

Cécile ran after them. She could barely hear Armand now. She knew it was getting late. She felt her heart pumping wildly in her chest, a sharp pain piercing her side. She grabbed her side and kept running. She could not let the children get away this time. They had Tante Tay's necklace. She was sure of it.

She noticed that buildings along the street were spaced farther and farther apart now. The street was turning into a dirt road. She saw the children run past the last house on the road. Up ahead was marsh.

Cécile realized she was getting close to the cypress swamps, and panic seeped into every muscle of her body. She slowed, frightened and gasping for breath. She could no longer hear Armand. Ahead, she couldn't see anything but reeds and grasses, standing water, and a few tall trees poking up from the marsh. The air smelled different—rich and dank, swampy. Beyond was the dark outline of the cypress forest.

Cécile stood still, her heart feeling as though it were trying to escape her chest. Where had the children gone? The marsh was silent except for grasses moving in the breeze and the sharp call of a bird.

Then Cécile thought she heard faint whispers coming from behind a stand of ancient-looking cypress trees a little way down the path. She tiptoed closer. The huge, gnarled cypress roots spread out into the marsh like a great rumpled skirt.

Peering around the trees, she saw the two children bent down among the roots, grasping a large root as if they were going to pry it out of the earth. To Cécile's amazement, the root lifted, and the children turned it over. Cécile saw that it was hollowed out. With one smooth movement, the children pushed the root out into the marsh. It was a boat! The boy grabbed paddles that had been hidden under the boat and hopped in.

"Mon Dieu," Cécile breathed.

Both children quickly turned, looking around, their eyes wide.

Cécile called to them, "Please don't worry. The police stopped chasing you blocks ago. It's only me, the girl on the elephant. I just want to get my necklace back."

The girl straightened. With sure steps, she scampered across the cypress roots toward Cécile. She reached into her cloak, and when she withdrew her hand, it was clenched around something. Cécile could see that the girl had a ring on every finger.

The girl stepped closer. "Here," she said. She opened her hand, her silver rings flashing in the setting sun. In her palm lay Tante Tay's cameo necklace, nestled in its circle of black lace.

Cécile started to reach for the necklace, but

then stopped. Had the children hoped to trade it for clothes, or food to eat?

"Do you need something for it?" Cécile stammered.

The girl shook her head. "The necklace isn't ours to trade," she said. Her French was rough, Cécile noticed, like the French spoken by some slaves and people who lived in the bayous upriver.

The boy who had saved Cécile from the elephant hopped out of the boat. He moved it back under the tree and flipped it over. Once again, it appeared to be only another cypress root.

The girl said, "We saw you wearing the necklace before you fell. The back part was broken."

The boy added, "We've been trying to give it back to you. But you're always someplace where the police like to chase us."

*That's true*, Cécile thought. Hadn't she seen the children coming toward her on the wharf on Saturday night, and again when she was riding the elephant? And even in Congo Square, they had been coming to her.

"Here," the girl said again. She reached out, and her thin fingers brushed Cécile's as she set the necklace in her hand.

Cécile saw that it looked exactly as it had when she'd taken it from its velvet box. She turned it over. "But it isn't broken," she said.

"I fixed it for you," the boy replied with a shy smile.

"Merci. Thank you so very much," Cécile said, fighting back tears. She stretched out a hand to the girl. "Forgive my manners. My name is Cécile Rey."

The girl did not take Cécile's hand, but she smiled. "I am Abena, and my brother's name is Caimon."

"We must go now," Caimon said. "It'll soon be dark in the forest." He pointed his chin toward the cypress swamp looming beyond the marsh.

*So they do live in the swamps,* Cécile thought. Monsieur John had been right about that. "Do you live there with your family?" she asked.

Abena nodded. "Our mother escaped from

slavery with us when we were very young. She has passed on now, but the others take care of us," she said. "They are our family."

"Do you trade at the French Market with the Old Goat Man?" Cécile asked. She didn't want to be rude, but she had so many questions.

Caimon nodded. "You mean Philippe, the butcher."

Cécile didn't know if her next question would make the children uncomfortable, but she had to know. "Are you maroons?"

Caimon smiled again. "Some call us that." He glanced again toward the setting sun. "Now we've got to go."

"Just one more thing," Cécile said. "I never had the chance to thank you for saving me from the elephant. Merci. I was so scared."

Abena said, "All animals love Caimon. They will do anything he asks." She paused. "Many of our people have a way with animals. One of our leaders can even call alligators."

Cécile reached out her hand to Abena. "Good-bye," she said.

Abena and Caimon looked at each other. After a minute, Abena took Cécile's hand, and then Caimon did the same.

Caimon and Abena walked down the path toward the forest of cypress trees. Cécile was puzzled.

"Wait," she called. "Why aren't you taking your boat?"

Abena and Caimon exchanged a glance before turning back to Cécile. "Come over here," Caimon said, motioning for her to follow with a wave of his hand. Silver rings flashed on his fingers, too.

They returned to the stand of cypress trees. Abena squatted and pointed to the small wooden boat that looked as if it were just another root.

Abena smiled gently. "If the police had come, then we would have taken the boat. We leave it here in case any of our people need to escape quickly back into the swamp. Look." Reaching into a little niche carved into the side of the boat, she lifted out what appeared to be the curved horn of an ox and showed Cécile a small hole at one end. "If we blow this horn, its sound carries far into the swamp. Then our people know that someone is in trouble, and they come to help."

The old woman's voice echoed in Cécile's mind: *Hunters want to kill lions . . . Lions only want to eat.* Now Cécile understood those words. Abena's people did only what they had to do to find food and stay free, yet they were hunted.

Abena set the horn back in its hiding place. "Don't tell anyone," she said.

"I won't," Cécile said. "I promise."

A voice rang out over the marsh. "Cécile! Cécé, where are you? Cécile!" It was Armand calling.

"We must go," Abena said.

Watching Caimon and Abena disappear down the path toward the cypress forest, Cécile felt an ache spreading in her chest. She wanted to know more about the children. She wished they could be friends. But she knew that wouldn't happen. Hidden away deep in the swamps, they were the ones she could not know.

# 14
## HANNAH'S SECRET

That night, Cécile waited in her bed until she was sure that everyone was asleep. Then she tiptoed into Tante Tay's room. She took the velvet box from the dresser and, with a deep sigh, placed the necklace back inside.

The mystery of who had picked up her necklace had been solved. It had not been taken by the man selling orange buns, or the circus performer carrying the fancy doggy purse, or Madame Irène, or Agnès Metoyer, who, as it turned out, had truly admired something of Cécile's for once. The two maroon children had picked up the necklace only to give it back to her in good faith.

Cécile closed her eyes and asked for blessings for the children to keep them safe. Then she prayed for Madame Irène, who had been right about everything.

When Cécile woke the next morning, she pulled open her drapes, and sunlight streamed into her room. She smiled, thinking happily, "Tante Tay will be home tomorrow!" How good it felt to be able to look forward to her aunt's homecoming again. Down in the courtyard, she heard Maman talking with Mathilde. They were probably making plans to welcome Tante Tay and little René home. Cécile wanted to help.

As she stepped from her room, she found a surprise outside her door. It was a little hand-woven bag with white lace trim and small pink flowers. It matched her new party dress.

Cécile walked over and picked it up. It had the most beautiful, delicate scent she had ever smelled.

Cécile hurried to the courtyard to see if Maman had made it for her. She almost bumped into Armand, who was walking down the stairs with a huge smile on his face.

"Good morning," Cécile said.

"Yes, it is, isn't it?" Armand replied cheerfully.

Cécile thought he was practically beaming. "What makes you so happy today?"

Armand just shrugged and continued ambling down the stairs, seemingly lost in dreamy thoughts. Realizing that she wasn't going to get an answer, Cécile raced past him to join Maman and Mathilde, seated at the courtyard's breakfast table. They were making a list—probably a menu for tomorrow's welcome dinner.

"Maman!" Cécile said, holding out the sweet-smelling sachet. "Did you make this for me? It's so lovely!"

Maman looked up, surprised. "Why, no—no, I didn't, but I just found a tin of tea on my writing desk. It smells exactly like the tea that helped my headache so quickly the other night."

Mathilde said, "And I found a jar of ointment on the kitchen windowsill this morning. It's for my joints. Hannah had me try it once before. I put some on my knees, and Lord, my pain was gone." The cook looked around the court-yard. "Where is Hannah? Have you seen her today?"

"No," Maman said. "Have you, Cécile?"

Cécile shook her head. "Usually she opens my drapes before I wake up. This morning she didn't come. Do you think she left us these gifts?"

Armand walked up. His smile was gone, and Cécile thought he looked as poorly as on the day he'd fainted from yellow fever.

"I found jars of paints by my door—incred-ible paints made from fruits, vegetables, leaves, flowers. There are colors I have never seen in paint. Until just now, I thought I was the only one who'd gotten a gift."

Maman and Mathilde exchanged worried looks.

A sinking feeling was grabbing Cécile. "Has Hannah left us?" she asked.

"Mathilde, come with me," Maman said. The two women rushed to the servants' quarters above the kitchen, Cécile and Armand right behind them.

Maman threw open Hannah's door. The small room was empty except for a neatly made bed, a chair, and a pitcher and basin on a side table. There were no clothes, no comb and brush, no keepsakes. Hannah was gone, leaving nothing behind except for the small gifts.

"But why? Why would she have left without a word?" Maman asked.

"She was doing a fine job here," Armand said. "She seemed happy with us."

Cécile held out hope. "Maybe," she said, "Hannah has just gone to visit her family, or her friends."

"Why would she take everything she owns and leave us all gifts?" Armand said.

"Do you know any of her friends, Mathilde?" Cécile asked.

Mathilde shook her head. "Not a soul I know admits to knowing her."

"How strange," Maman murmured. "She surely knows Monsieur Lejeune. She told me that he suggested she ask us for work."

Suddenly Cécile's mind flashed back to her conversation with Hannah as they had walked to the tea party just the day before.

"She does know Monsieur Lejeune," Cécile said slowly. "I saw them talking together in Jackson Square last Sunday. But—but yesterday, I asked Hannah about him, and she said that she'd never heard of him."

Cécile swallowed a lump rising in her throat. She felt sure that Hannah was in some kind of trouble. Otherwise, she wouldn't have lied or left the Reys without a word.

Cécile looked at Armand's wrinkled brow. He appeared to be worried, too.

"Come on, Cécé," Armand said urgently. "Perhaps Monsieur Lejeune knows something. We'll go talk to him now."

Cécile and Armand sped toward Monsieur Lejeune's home. Armand banged on the door.

Monsieur Lejeune called through the door, "Who is it?"

Armand told him.

A moment passed before Monsieur Lejeune opened the door. "Good morning, Armand, Cécile. May I help—" Then he stopped mid-sentence. "What has happened? Are you all right?"

"May we come in?" Armand asked.

Monsieur Lejeune peered over Armand's shoulder. "Are you alone?" Cécile had never seen her tutor so unnerved.

"Of course we are." Armand shoved past him.

"Armand!" Cécile cried out.

Monsieur held up his hand. "It's all right, it's all right. Come in, Cécile." He closed and locked the door behind them.

"I think you're aware that Hannah has left our house," Armand began, his voice tight. "Tell us what is going on."

The two men studied each other.

"If she is in some difficulty, we want to help. That's all," Armand said. "Please, tell us what you know."

Monsieur Lejeune nodded once. "I will not tell you where she is, but I promise you that she is safe, at least for now."

"What do you mean, she's safe?" Armand asked, almost in a whisper. "Safe from what?"

Monsieur Lejeune cleared his throat. "I did not want to involve you and your family. You must believe that." He paused. "A slave trader has put up handbills for Hannah all around New Orleans. Yesterday she saw a slave dealer questioning one of your neighbors. She had to leave quickly—for her safety, and your family's, also."

"I don't understand," Cécile said. "Hannah could just show her papers, couldn't she, Armand?"

"*Is* Hannah a slave?" Armand asked Monsieur Lejeune, sounding much calmer than Cécile felt.

"The short answer is yes. She *was* free, but she was forced back into slavery in Virginia."

A chill gripped Cécile's body. She could not stop her hands from shaking, recalling Armand's encounter with slave catchers. Another memory flashed into her mind—Hannah disappearing from sight yesterday just as Cécile saw the slave catcher pulling the slave along. Cécile caught her breath: Hannah hadn't reappeared until the slave catcher was out of sight.

Was this Hannah's secret—that she was a slave running from slave catchers? Was that why she had dressed so strangely to go outside? Why she had walked with her head lowered and her shawl almost covering her face? Why no one Mathilde knew had ever heard of her? And was this the reason Hannah had understood so well when Cécile needed to keep her own secret about the gloves and Tante Tay's necklace? What had Hannah said then? *Sometimes even when we don't want to, we must keep secrets . . .*

"Hannah was sold here in New Orleans last year," Monsieur Lejeune was explaining now, "but her new owner, Talbot, beat her every day. She escaped, and people put her in touch with my sister and me. We took her in."

"So you and Mademoiselle Lejeune help

runaways? It's a brave thing you are doing," Armand said.

Stunned, Cécile looked at her tutor as if she had never really seen him before. Monsieur Lejeune and his sister were well known in New Orleans society. Cécile couldn't imagine them helping slaves escape. Every free person of color knew that helping a slave escape was punishable by death.

Monsieur brushed Armand's compliment aside. "Since people are in and out of our home frequently, we thought it best that Hannah stay someplace else. I knew your good family needed a maid." He paused. "We didn't think Talbot would look for her here in New Orleans. We thought he'd assume that she ran north. We had no intention of putting your family or any other family in danger."

"What will happen to her now?" Armand demanded.

"We have been trying to get Hannah out of New Orleans, but right now it is impossible," Monsieur Lejeune replied. "We are keeping her hidden until something can be arranged. But with those handbills everywhere and slave catchers closing in—"

"How can we help?" Armand asked.

Again, Monsieur Lejeune studied Armand, as if assessing how far he could trust him. "If you truly wish to help, go home. Speak of this to no one but your family. Be sure that every hint of Hannah's presence is removed from your home. If anyone asks, act as if you and your family have never met her. Don't come here again, unless you absolutely must."

Armand nodded and said softly, "Good-bye, monsieur. Please tell Hannah that the Rey family will do everything we can to protect her."

On their way home, Cécile and Armand walked in silence. Finally, when they were nearly home, Armand asked Cécile to help him burn his painting. "It's the only thing left to show that she was in our house," he said.

Cécile's head jerked up in surprise. She tried to remember the half-finished painting she had seen in the dusky courtyard. The portrait had reminded her of someone, hadn't it? She just hadn't recognized Hannah dressed in the fashions of a fine lady.

It was one more thing she hadn't noticed. Cécile hadn't even recognized the signs that her brother was smitten with Hannah. Was that because she'd been so worried about the necklace? Or was it more than that?

Armand interrupted her thoughts. "You know, Cécé, I never had the chance to really talk to Hannah. But she was so graceful, so smart and kind. And she had the gift of finding beauty in the smallest things."

Cécile knew that her brother's heart was breaking. She squeezed his hand.

Armand said, "Sometimes I wish we could avoid seeing all the meanness in the world."

Like a whisper in the trees, Cécile heard Madame Irène's words. *Open your eyes so you can see.*

# THE CAMEO NECKLACE

Was this what Madame Irène had meant? Until the last few days, Cécile had been blind to all the things around her that happened to people of color. When she had thought about people of color, she'd thought only of people like herself, the *gens de couleur libres*, the free people of color; she had rarely thought about slaves, and certainly not maroons. She touched the paper in her pocket, the only thing that kept her free. It seemed very fragile now. According to Monsieur Lejeune, Hannah had once been free. Only a few days ago, Armand could have been put into slavery if he hadn't had his papers with him.

Cécile's body shivered. Her eyes were opening, but Armand was right—she wasn't sure she wanted to see.

Cécile wished that she had never taken the cameo necklace. She had seen and learned so many hard lessons since then.

She heard Madame Irène's voice whisper again: *Open your eyes so you can see.*

# 15
## SHADOWS IN THE NIGHT

That night, Cécile dreamed that she was riding bareback on a great black horse. All she could hear was the thunder of the horse's hooves. The pounding of the hooves became so loud, she could feel the vibration in her body.

Cécile sat up in bed. She heard the banging loudly now. It was real, and it was coming from downstairs. Someone was beating on the door.

She heard her father and grandfather talking to each other downstairs. Then she heard men shouting commands.

She slipped on her robe and ran into the hall. Armand had just come out of his room, already dressed, and had gone to the top of the stairs.

Cécile said, "What's happening? Who is it, Armand?"

She could hear her father's voice booming, and Grand-père's raised in measured protest.

Armand said, "Get dressed. Hurry."

Cécile raced into her room, quickly putting on her clothes, and hurried back into the hall.

"They're slave catchers," Armand whispered, grabbing Cécile's hand. "We need to warn Monsieur Lejeune. Let's go." He led the way toward the courtyard stairs.

Once they were outside, Armand signaled that they would climb over the fence behind the huge cistern where rainwater collected. He climbed over first and waited to catch Cécile.

They raced toward the Lejeunes' house in the darkness. As she ran, Cécile saw Madame Irène's face in her mind. A strange and hopeful idea began to take shape.

Breathless, Cécile and Armand pounded on the Lejeunes' door. It seemed to open instantly. Monsieur Lejeune was in his robe. Looking past them both right and left, he said, "Come in quickly."

"Slave catchers." Armand was panting so hard that he was barely able to get words out. "They're at our house, looking for Hannah. I fear they may come here next."

Monsieur Lejeune blanched. "We have her well hidden here, but the danger is great."

"Monsieur?" Cécile said. "I know a safe place for her."

Cécile's tutor and brother turned to her in surprise.

"Where is it?" Mademoiselle Lejeune asked urgently. Monsieur's sister stepped into the room, her eyes puffy with sleep. Behind her, Hannah appeared, already dressed.

"I know where you can go, Hannah," Cécile said, running to hug her around the waist. "There are maroons in the swamps who will keep you safe. I know how to find them."

Monsieur Lejeune looked shocked. "How on earth do you know this, Cécile? And the swamps—mon Dieu! That's out of the question;

that is a dangerous and inhospitable place."

"Monsieur, Cécile is telling the truth," Armand said. "And yes, the swamps are inhospitable—they are uninviting and scary enough that slave catchers won't enter. There is no safer place for Hannah now."

Monsieur Lejeune began to protest again, but Hannah stopped him. "I'll go," she said.

"But the alligators—" Monsieur began.

Cécile said, "I made friends with some maroon children. I know how to find them, and I'm sure they could get Hannah safely to the others tonight."

As Monsieur Lejeune continued to protest, Cécile thought about why it was that Hannah had to leave. There was no doubt in Cécile's mind that slavery wasn't fair or right. Yet people who wanted only to be free were chased and hunted. Again she heard the whisper of Madame Irène's voice in her mind. *Open your eyes so you can see.*

"We're wasting time," Armand said loudly, jolting Cécile from her thoughts.

# SHADOWS IN THE NIGHT

Cécile, Armand, Hannah, and Monsieur Lejeune made their way through the dark streets, all four of them swallowed up in the silent shadows of the night.

They followed the dirt road Cécile had taken before. She led the way into the marsh, trying to remember where the children had turned off onto the path that led toward the cypress forest. Everything looked different in the dark.

Finally, Cécile found the path and followed it to the stand of ancient cypress trees, their gnarled, gigantic roots extending into the water. She stopped, relieved. The others waited as she climbed carefully over the spreading roots, feeling for the one dark shape that was not a root but a boat. Her heart thudded. What if a snake or an alligator was lurking near the boat? What if this was not the right stand of trees? What if someone else in trouble had already taken the boat tonight?

Finally, a shape moved and rocked at her touch. Softly, she called Armand and Monsieur

Lejeune. They turned the boat over, setting it in the shallow water that lapped at the edge of the marsh. Silently, Armand and Monsieur Lejeune picked up the paddles, stepped into the boat, and assisted Hannah and Cécile.

In the dim light, Cécile searched for the carved niche that held the horn. There! She lifted it out and showed the others. A cord was attached to it, and Cécile slipped it around her neck.

Monsieur Lejeune said quietly, "Don't blow the horn yet. We're still too close to the city. We must paddle a ways into the swamp."

Suddenly, there was a rustling in the trees. Monsieur Lejeune held his finger to his mouth, signaling that they should remain quiet. All of them held their breath and waited. Had a slave catcher followed them here? Cécile felt sweat tickling her lip, but she dared not move to wipe it off.

The rustling began again, louder this time. Cécile heard movement through the thick reeds. She stopped breathing.

The sound came closer. Cécile turned her head to look. Coming out into the clearing was a beady-eyed possum, its eyes shiny in the darkness.

Cécile heard the others sigh with relief, but she still felt terrified. "You're right, monsieur, we are too close," she whispered. "Let's go."

Armand and Monsieur Lejeune lifted the paddles, gently pushing the boat into deeper water. They moved slowly through the dense marsh, making only the smallest sounds as the paddles slid in and out of the water. No one spoke.

The moonlight grew fainter as they entered the cypress forest. Cécile saw vines and moss drooping from the tall trees, looking like ghosts ready to pounce at any second. A foul smell filled her nose. Bugs buzzed around her head, biting and stinging. Broken trees jutted up out of the water like elephant trunks. The cypress trees were so wide at the bottom, they looked as if they wore women's skirts. Small patches of fog clung to the water, like smoke lifting up from a fire. Cécile knew the vast cypress forest had stood sentry over the swamp for eons. Sounds were everywhere—frogs, katydids, birds, and other, unknown sounds. Sometimes Cécile thought she saw eyes peering out from the trees and the water.

Even breathing seemed different. Air did not fill Cécile's lungs the same way it did outside the swamp. She felt as if she might be suffocating. She heard plopping sounds in the water and wondered if water snakes or alligators were swimming near.

Cécile wasn't sure whether minutes or hours had passed when Monsieur Lejeune stopped paddling. "I think we've gone far enough," he said. "Any farther, and I'm not sure we can find our way back."

"Cécé, it's time," Armand said. "Try your horn."

Cécile lifted the horn and put it to her mouth. She blew into it. Nothing, not a sound.

Cécile was shaking. She blew again. Nothing.

"I'll try if you want me to," Armand said.

Cécile shook her head and closed her eyes. She blew again, harder this time. The horn blasted. Cécile blew three more times. The sound of the horn seemed to belong to the swamp, blending in with all the splashing, croaking, squawking sounds. Cécile blew the horn again.

"How will they find us?" Hannah said.

"I don't know," Cécile replied. "I just believe they will."

They sat, quietly waiting. Cécile prayed that the two children would come soon, before daybreak, before alligators or slave catchers set upon them.

The moon appeared overhead, breaking through the thick canopy of trees. Cécile scanned the water's edge, where she saw a clump of lavender flowers. It seemed strange to see such beauty out here in this place. She felt strengthened by the flowers' loveliness and called out, hoping the children could hear her, "It's me—your friend Cécile."

As she waited for an answer, she heard

Hannah gasp. Armand pointed.

Cécile followed Armand's gaze. She froze. Six pairs of yellowish, triangular eyes looked at them, slowly moving toward the boat. Alligators!

Then from nowhere she heard it, the most ancient of sounds—the sound you might hear if the earth itself decided to speak. The alligators stopped moving toward the boat. One by one, they turned and disappeared under the water. Cécile remembered Abena saying that one of their leaders could call alligators.

Monsieur Lejeune tapped Cécile's hand and nodded toward the closest bank. A man who must have made the strange sound waded out into the reeds toward them. Cécile tightened her fingers around the horn. He didn't know them; would he think them enemies? Cécile was about to call for Abena and Caimon when she heard Caimon's voice.

"It's all right," he called to her. She saw him standing on the bank where the man had been. "We're here." Cécile didn't see Abena, but she knew the girl was there, keeping a watchful eye.

Armand and Monsieur Lejeune guided the boat toward the bank. Cécile explained Hannah's situation.

"She can find safety with us," the man said. He reached out and pulled the boat ashore. The group stepped out of the boat.

Cécile said good-bye to Hannah. She could barely see Hannah's face through her tears.

"Thank you, Cécile," Hannah whispered. "I will always hold you in my heart."

Cécile flung her arms around Hannah. "I don't want you to leave, Hannah," she whispered. But she knew that Hannah had to leave, or she would surely spend the rest of her life in slavery.

When Cécile loosened her arms and let Hannah go, she knew that she had found something more valuable than the cameo necklace— she had found her heart. She could feel it breaking now.

Cécile watched as Hannah hugged Monsieur Lejeune. Last, she hugged Armand and gave him a gentle kiss on his cheek.

The man pushed the boat back into the murky water. Armand and Monsieur Lejeune climbed in and helped Cécile. All on the boat watched as Caimon took Hannah's hand. In a moment, Caimon and Hannah, the man, and Abena had all disappeared into the mists of the swamp.

Cécile felt salty tears on her lips. She dared not look at her brother. *What sorrow slavery brings,* Cécile thought, *and what awful choices we must make for freedom.*

It didn't take long for Armand and Monsieur Lejeune to paddle the boat out of the swamp and back to the cypress trees where Cécile had found it. As she stepped from the boat, the moon broke through the clouds again, lighting up the spot where they stood.

Cécile looked out on the marsh, its grasses and stagnant water silvery in the moonlight. She turned her head in one direction, toward the city, and then in the other, toward the dark silhouette of the cypress forest. She thought of the old woman's words: *Open your eyes so you can see.*

Since Cécile had first heard those words, her eyes had opened to much that was painful, sad, and frightening in the world . . . but she was not sorry. How else could she have seen Hannah's trouble, or known how to help her?

The old woman, Madame Irène, had known Cécile would open her eyes to the world around her and open her heart to Hannah. She marveled at how the loss of Tante Tay's necklace had led her to the children, who had then led Hannah to safety. Everything in the world, she thought, was like an intricate, delicate piece of lace, woven together like a fine shawl.

Cécile saw the old woman's face in her mind. Now Madame Irène was smiling, and this time, so was Cécile.

# LOOKING BACK

# A PEEK INTO THE PAST

*A cypress swamp in Louisiana*

Just as Cécile discovers in the story, people called *maroons* really did live in hidden settlements deep in the swamps near New Orleans.

Even today, the vast swamps are dangerous and hard to navigate. Cypress trees draped in Spanish moss block out the sun. Quicksand and dense vegetation make walking treacherous. Alligators and poisonous snakes live in the mazelike waterways.

Yet in the 1700s and 1800s, these very dangers offered safety to escaping slaves, because slave catchers rarely ventured into such forbidding places.

Enslaved men first became familiar with the swamps because they were forced to work there, cutting down cypress trees for their valuable wood. Over time, many went deeper into the swamps, beyond the reach of overseers and slave owners. In the most hidden, hard-to-reach places, they built cabins for their families, hunted and fished, and planted gardens of corn, sweet potatoes, and squash. Maroon communities sometimes lasted for generations.

*Hiding out in the swamps*

Although they lived in hidden settlements, maroons were not cut off from society. Using the natural resources available in the swamps, they made goods to trade, including cypress logs, sassafras tea, and cypress or palmetto baskets. Going cautiously into nearby villages and even into New Orleans, they traded these items for money, flour, sugar, guns and

*A cypress basket*

*The French Market in New Orleans*

gunpowder, clothes, and other things they could not make themselves. They stayed in touch with enslaved friends and relatives and sometimes helped other slaves escape. Sometimes they slipped onto nearby plantations and stole food or other necessities.

Many people knew that maroons existed. Some considered them modern-day Robin Hoods, stealing from the rich and helping the poor. But others—especially slave owners—hated and feared maroons, seeing them as out-laws and troublemakers.

Sometimes the government sent soldiers into the swamps to catch maroons and destroy their settlements. In the 1780s, a maroon leader named San Malo was caught and publicly hanged in New Orleans. In the 1830s, soldiers killed a maroon named Bras-Coupé and left his body on display in New Orleans' public square. In Cécile's time, police probably kept a close eye on anyone suspected of being a maroon, like the boy and girl she meets in the story.

Maroons were not unique to Louisiana. The word "maroon" comes from the Spanish word *cimarrón*, meaning cattle or horses that escape into the wild. Eventually it was also used for escaped slaves who chose to live free in remote places rather than risk capture, slavery, and prejudice.

Although few Americans today have heard of maroons, their hidden communities existed all through the South. From Virginia to Florida and west to Louisiana, maroons made their homes in swamps. In Texas, they lived in mountains and deserts. In fact, maroon settlements sprang up wherever people were enslaved, including the Caribbean and

*In Florida, maroons escaped into the Everglades and joined with the Seminole Indians. Today, people with this mixed heritage are known as "Black Seminoles."*

*This Jamaican bill honors a maroon woman of the Caribbean.*

Central and South America. Whether maroons settled in jungles, swamps, mountains, or deserts, they shared a desire to live freely by their own rules.

By Cécile's time, however, thousands of free black people were living in American cities and towns. About 10,000 free people of color lived in New Orleans in the 1850s. In the years before the Civil War, though, racial tensions rose sharply, making life more difficult and dangerous. For example, free people of color

*A free girl of color, and the courtyard of a New Orleans home*

were required to carry papers proving that they were legally free. People caught without papers were in terrible danger of being enslaved. Some managed to prove their freedom in court, but most were shipped hundreds of miles up the Mississippi River and sold into slavery. In most

*A New Orleans man carried this paper for years to prove that he was legally free.*

cases, their families never knew what had happened to them.

Despite such risks, free people of color still enjoyed the rich cultural life and entertainments in New Orleans—theaters, operas, cafés, churches, markets, and more. The *Floating Palace* showboat came to New Orleans every winter, bringing a marvelous circus. In an era before movies and television, a circus—with tightrope artists, acrobats, and trained animals performing before a live audience—was an amazing and heart-stopping spectacle for a girl like Cécile.

*A circus performance on the elegant Floating Palace showboat*

# GLOSSARY OF FRENCH WORDS

**au revoir** *(oh ruh-vwar)*—good-bye

**bonjour** *(bohn-zhoor)*—hello

**chérie** *(shay-ree)*—dear, darling

**gens de couleur libres** *(zhahn duh koo-luhr lee-bruh)*—
free people of color

**ma chérie** *(mah shay-ree)*—my dear, my darling

**madame** *(mah-dahm)*—Mrs., ma'am

**mademoiselle** *(mahd-mwah-zel)*—Miss, young lady

**marchand** *(mar-shahn)*—a male seller or merchant

**marchande** *(mar-shahnd)*—a female seller or merchant

**merci** *(mehr-see)*—thank you

**mon Dieu** *(mohn-dyuh)*—good heavens; my God

**monsieur** *(muh-syuh)*—Mister, sir

**non** *(nohn)*—no

**oui** *(wee)*—yes

**pardon** *(par-dohn)*—excuse me, pardon me

**tante** *(tahnt)*—aunt

**tignon** *(tee-yohn)*—a scarf or kerchief tied around the head;
often worn by women of color in Louisiana

**très bien** *(treh byen)*—very good

# HOW TO PRONOUNCE FRENCH NAMES

**Agnès Metoyer** *(ah-nyess meh-twah-yay)*

**Armand** *(ar-mahn)*

**Aurélia** *(oh-ray-lyah)*

**Bras-Coupé** *(bra–koo-pay)*—Cut Arm, One-Armed Man

**Cécé** *(say-say)*

**Cécile Rey** *(say-seel ray)*

**Cochon** *(koh-shohn)*

**Grand-père** *(grahn-pehr)*—Grandpa, Grandfather

**Irène** *(ee-ren)*

**Jean-Claude** *(zhahn-klohd)*

**Lejeune** *(luh-zhun)*

**Maman** *(mah-mahn)*—Mama, Mother

**Mathilde** *(mah-tild)*

**Monette Bruiller** *(moh-net brew-yay)*

**Octavia** *(ohk-tah-vyah)*

**Philippe** *(fee-leep)*

**Pierre** *(pyehr)*

**René** *(ruh-nay)*

# AUTHOR'S NOTE

Thanks to Denise Lewis Patrick for creating the character of Cécile Rey.

Thanks to Dr. Gwendolyn Midlo Hall, author, historian, and renowned professor, and to authors and New Orleans natives Freddi Evans, who wrote *Congo Square: African Roots in New Orleans*, and Keith Weldon Medley, who told me about Bras-Coupé, for all their assistance during my trip to New Orleans and my research efforts. Thanks to John Hankins, executive director of the New Orleans African American Museum of Art, Culture and History. Thanks also to the staff of the Historic New Orleans Collection and Williams Research Center, especially research assistants Eric Seiferth and Jennifer Navarre, and the staff of the Hermann-Grima & Gallier Historic Houses in New Orleans for making sure I understood the historical context of the time. Thanks also to maroon descendant Phil Fixico for all the information he passed along to me. A big thanks to the staff of the Auburn Avenue Research Library, especially Eleanor L. Hunter, reference librarian; Angela Ahmad, library associate; and Kerrie Cotten Williams, archivist, for their assistance in helping me locate books and photos; and to Morris Gardner, program division manager, for making sure I had a place to work. I would be remiss not to thank Captain Jay Boutte of the Louisiana Swamp Tours for his knowledge and for allowing me to hold his year-old alligator. Yikes!

Love and thanks to my mother, Annie S. Coleman; my brother, Edward J. Coleman; my aunts, Audrey White (who gave me my iPad), Lucille Mendez Vaz, and Swannie Richards; my granddaughter, Taylor 7 Blayne Parker; my grandson, Jody Santana Rhone; my eldest daughter, Travara Mueed Strigl; my new son-in-law, Matthew Strigl; and my adopted daughter, Gina Barboza.

In addition, I want to give a special thanks to American Girl marketing manager Mary Guenther, who saved the day; historian Mark Speltz, for working diligently to keep me on the right track throughout my research for this book; my editor and dear friend, Peg Ross, without whom I could not have finished; and my daughter, Latrayan (Sankofa) Mueed, for refusing to let me stop.

And lastly, even though he has no idea he helped me, I'd like to thank Grandpa Elliott, New Orleans street musician who is now with the marvelous Playing for Change Band, for inspiring me through his music.

# About the Author

Evelyn Coleman grew up in North Carolina with her parents and brother, surrounded by a large extended family. Today, she lives in Atlanta, Georgia, with her husband and enjoys spending time with her two grandchildren.

She is the author of *Shadows on Society Hill: An Addy Mystery*, which was a finalist for the Edgar Award, and many other award-winning books for children and young adults.